Love Before Time: Lucifer and Gabriel

Balance Series #6

By Lisa Oliver

Love Before Time: Lucifer and Gabriel (Balance Series #6)

piracy of copyrighted material. Your support of the author's rights and livelihood is appreciated.

Love Before Time: Lucifer and Gabriel is a work of fiction. Names, characters, places and incidents are either the product of the author's imagination or are used fictitiously and any resemblance to any actual persons, living or dead, events or locales is entirely coincidental. All trademarks are owned by the relevant companies and are used for reference purposes in this book only.

Table of Contents

Dedication
Let Love and Peace Win

Prologue

Lucifer was fully recovered, but he liked having Gabriel there as his own personal caregiver. Thus, he pretended to be convalescing longer than he needed to.

"Gabe, be a darling, and hand me that water cup, please?"

Gabriel, who was sitting on the sofa across the office, reading a banned book of essays by *Walter Benjamin*.

"It's right there, Luc. You can't reach it yourself?" he asked with strained but seemingly endless patience for the patient.

"Feeling a bit weak today," Lucifer moaned. "But I'll try, I guess."

Gabriel watched as the Lord of the Underworld lifted his hand within an inch of the glass, then let it fall.

"Honestly," he sighed. "That hard, is it?"

"You have no idea," Lucifer said as he licked his dry lips, searching desperately for some moisture.

"Fine," the archangel sighed as he marked his page, stood reluctantly up, walked towards the side table, and handed the cup of water over.

"Can you bend the straw, please?"

"Don't push it," Gabriel admonished as he tilted the plastic straw down on a forty-five-degree angle. "You're sure you're not feeling better? I distinctly recalled Raphael saying that you should be right as rain in a few days. That was over a week ago."

"He's a healer, Gabriel, not a fucking physician," Lucifer replied. "If you've better things to do, I can always get that cute little Ariago here. He's more than qualified to minister to my every need."

"No, no. I said I'd care for you until you're back on your feet, and I meant it." Gabriel pulled a chair beside the bed. "Comfortable? Need another pillow or anything?"

"Very comfortable"

"Hungry?"

"I'm good, thanks."

"TV? Movie? A game of Scrabble, perhaps?"

"No, no, Gabe. You can go back to your book."

"You're sure?"

"Totally. Maybe I'll nap."

"Very well."

Gabriel waited a moment. When there was still only silence emanating from Lucifer, he stood, replaced the chair to its original spot, crossed back to the sofa, sank into its plush leather cushion, and opened his book.

He wasn't half a page in when his charge spoke once more.

"I recognized him, you know."

Gabriel looked up. "Who? Malphas?"

Lucifer nodded. "Not by how he looked, of course, but the feeling in the room. He was with us, I'm sure, way back in the day. He was one of us."

Gabriel closed the book and asked the question that had been burning inside of him since he'd learned of Lucifer being taken down.

"What happened, Luc? How did he manage to lay you out for so long and come so close to ending your existence entirely? I didn't think it was possible."

Lucifer pulled himself up in the bed. "I don't know for sure. All I remember was coming back into my office after a long day and feeling exhausted. I tried to tell Carmine that I was going to have a nap, but he wasn't at his post. So, I came in here, laid down on that couch where you're sitting now, and must have drifted off. The next thing I knew, I opened my eyes with the worst headache I've ever known, and my office had been turned into a WWF cage match."

Gabriel nodded slowly at Lucifer's explanation. How Malphas gained access and drugged the Lord while he was asleep would clearly remain a mystery.

"Do you think there are any more of us out there?" Lucifer asked.

"Not according to Michael's debrief," Gabriel said. "Malphas himself eliminated the remaining beings leftover from that time. All that was left was us. After he finished with you, he was apparently going to come for me."

Lucifer looked long at Gabriel, considering the repercussions of a world without the two of them. He couldn't wrap his mind around the thought at all.

"Maybe I was a bit too hasty," he quietly mused, "sending him off to the pit like that. Should I have given him some time? Maybe a chance to change his ways?"

"I would have done the same if I was in your position," Gabriel said. "No point in second-guessing a choice like that in hindsight. What's done is done. Best to let it go and move on."

Lucifer smiled as he nodded but felt a bitter snake of a memory crawl up from his belly.

"Where have I heard that before," he said, more to himself than to his caregiver.

"Hmm?" Gabriel said, his nose already back in his book. "Heard what?"

"*Best to let it go and move on,*" Lucifer repeated, chewing on the words as he tried to find the source of the memory.

"I don't know," the archangel said. "Not an entirely uncommon phrase to say. You could have heard it any number of times."

Lucifer swung his legs around and stood up, his bare ass peeking out of the hospital gown Raphael insisted he wore if he was going to stay in bed.

"*You* said it." As soon as he said it, Lucifer knew it was true. "You said those words to *me.*"

Gabriel looked up again, his frustration

at being constantly interrupted starting to show. "It's entirely possible," he said, then added. "You look considerably better all of a sudden."

"Those were among your first words to me after all that shit went down with Head Office. After I was banished and fell so low. *Best to let it go*, you said. *And move on*."

Gabriel could sense the tension mounting in the room. "I might have done. Honestly, Luc, I don't recall."

"Well, I fucking do," Lucifer snapped. "I recall it all now. Seeing Malphas is bringing that whole forgotten puzzle back to me. Piece by shit-stained piece."

"Oh, for goodness sake," Gabriel said as he stood up. "Do you want to tell me what's going on? I have no idea what you're talking about or why you're so upset.

"Because you're still in the blissful state of denial," Lucifer replied. "A luxury I no longer have access to."

Gabriel was beginning to lose his long-practiced calm. "*Denial*? Denial of *what*? One minute you can't reach a fucking glass of water without me holding your hand, and the next, you're standing like a resurrected king, accusing me of saying something completely innocuous once upon a time. Maybe the drugs have caused you to have a stroke or aneurysm of some kind. A cyst on your brain tissue, perhaps? I don't know."

"My brain is just fine, Gabriel. It's yours that isn't functioning properly."

Gabriel pursed his lips and tucked the book under his arm. "Well then. You seem to be doing fine enough now. No need for me to stay here and be insulted."

As he walked briskly to the door, Lucifer's voice cut him deep and stopped him in his tracks.

"I loved you, Gabriel," the Prince of Darkness cried. "All that light back then. It was all for you. I loved you more than existence, more than I loved the Master Himself, and you broke my heart."

"I broke your heart? What did I do? You're the one who defied Head Office and refused to follow the Great Commandment. I, at least, took pity on you and sought you out after the fall. No one else came to visit, I seem to recall."

"You lied to me," Lucifer bellowed, his voice cracking with raw emotion. "I've buried that memory so deeply, but now I see it clear as day. You betrayed me. You betrayed my love. We had a promise, and you broke it, Gabriel. And by doing so, you broke my heart."

"Luc," Gabriel said with unmistakable compassion in his voice. "I don't know what you're talking about, but I can see it's hurting you terribly. Let me help you. I hate to see you in such pain."

Lucifer stood to his full height and opened his mouth in reply. He was more shocked than anyone to find the words that came out were the same as those spoken to him by the Master on that dark and terrible day.

"Get out of my sight!"

Gabriel was struck by Lucifer's commandment - stricken, in fact - knowing the full weight of the phrase better than anyone. Now wasn't the time to let his emotions show though. He left, as ordered, before the tears came.

Chapter One

For the first time in the forever of his existence, Gabriel felt pathetically human. He let the tears flow freely down his face until his eyes stung, and he could barely hold them open any longer. Somehow being banished from his one and only, his truth, his love, had bought him to his knees in the worst way, and he felt a pain so unimaginable that he never thought he could feel joy again.

Moping, brooding, thinking far too much... they were the traits of other people but now it was all he could do. Since Lucifer had uttered those fateful words, Gabriel felt as though the very fabric of who he was had been ripped in a way it couldn't be repaired, and he was suffering badly.

To name how he was feeling as heartbroken, depressed, or down in the dumps did not come close to the all-encompassing grief that wracked through him wave after hideous wave. He avoided working, didn't return communications from Head Office, and all but cut off contact with his angels. There was no release from this torment. He may as well have been in the

Underworld, not that he was allowed to set foot there.

It was worrying him to no end, and as much as Gabriel knew he should want to be free of his despair and depression, he couldn't shake it. He alternated between wallowing in his pain, and shouting in anger, always ensuring no one could hear him of course.

Because anger was a part of Gabriel's pain. He couldn't understand how Lucifer could treat him so cruelly. He was Archangel Gabriel, The Voice of the Master. He could flatten cities with a wave of his hand, he could fly around the world in one attempt and not even break a sweat. Gabriel was not egotistical, more of a realist. He knew that if Lucifer was so hurt that he had imposed banishment, then it was going to be an incredibly hard bridge to repair, and that meant accepting the very real possibility of a life without Lucifer in it.

And it was the pain of that truth - a life without Lucifer - that brought Gabriel to his knees. Because even before time it had always been him and Lucifer.

After the Fall, Gabriel had been patient. He had waited, knowing that Lucifer would be in his arms one day. It was destined, there was no one else, so it had to be Lucifer, if not now, then someday. That hope was now shattered in pieces that used to make up his heart, and he could not reconcile an existence without Lucifer in it.

In the meantime, Gabriel's staff floundered. Gabriel's pain – the way he cut off all contact with anyone was unprecedented. Some of his staff sent out an SOS to the higher-ranking angels, and one by one, they showed up to offer whatever help they could. But one by one, they left, with nothing changing. Nobody could get through the veil of despair that was blanketing Gabriel, because Gabriel himself didn't want them to.

Because to give up his heartbreak, give up on his suffering, would be, in his eyes, a betrayal of the person he'd always held most dear – the one who'd pushed him away in such a brutal fashion.

Lucifer.

The Prince of Darkness, Lord of Lies, King of the Underworld, was also to Gabriel if to no one else - the bringer of light and his one true love. Gabriel knew him and loved him - from a time before such titles and labels had been applied. From a time when they were young and together in bliss, part of an angelic cohort of like-minded beings who shared in ecstasy with them, long before man and all his complications came on the scene.

In hindsight, it felt like they had been mated then. They hadn't been, of course, not in any real or official sense of the word, but that's how it felt. But maybe that was just retrospection fucking with Gabriel's memory? A memory that he wished he could let go of as much as he wished he could recover it in total. Would he be in so much pain if he knew the truth of his own actions.

To Gabriel, at least, it felt like he was with Lucifer, and now he wasn't. Not that he had been officially mated to anyone before, but he could *imagine* what it was to feel bound to one and one only. There was no acknowledgment per se, and nothing was declared or paraded for others to see. In truth, before the concept of binaries and opposites was formulated, he and Lucifer and all the others were one. But for Gabriel, he had to admit, it had always been Lucifer. They had loved before love was a concept.

Yes, there were separate bodies, and they would enjoy the company of everybody in close proximity to their own. Not fucking. No sex was even required. Just being. Which, as far as Gabriel's memory told him, was far more satisfying and fulfilling than any amount of sucking or penetration could provide.

It was pure bliss. And like so many mortals were aware, a person might not ever understand how good something was until it was taken away. Even angels as wise and far-seeing as Gabriel could fall victim to the *Big Yellow Taxi* syndrome.

What hurt the most was Gabriel's understanding that Lucifer felt betrayed. Lucifer - the master of betrayal himself - felt betrayed by Gabriel. And the angel could not figure out why. No matter how hard Gabriel tried to conjure the memories from pre-time, he could not find the answers he was so desperately seeking. So, all he had left was speculation.

As he tried to lose himself in memories again, he considered the reasons Lucifer could have to feel what he felt. But a noise shook Gabriel out of his contemplation. It was a mountain of pizza boxes and beer cans tumbling over.

"Really?" Anael said as he stepped through the dumpster of Gabriel's office. "You've resorted to emotional eating and alcohol abuse?"

Gabriel shrugged without turning around.

"It's a pigsty in here," the Angel of Love said as he proceeded to stack boxes and fill a garbage bag with empty cans. "How can you live like this?"

Gabriel didn't care, he could handle one more angel judging him, but he couldn't bear the thought of one of them cleaning up after him. He would not stoop to that level. Without looking up, he lifted his index finger, and all the boxes and cans vanished. The place was instantly spotless.

"I'd ask if you're suffering from heartburn, but the boxes were clean, and the cans looked as if they came right off the factory conveyor belt. You haven't been eating or drinking anything, have you?"

Gabriel's lips pulled together in a pout. Anael was right: as an archangel he had no need for food or drink but he liked the *idea* of indulging in unhealthy pursuits to salve his aching soul.

"Regardless of whether you have been indulging in earthly solace or not, you look like shit," Anael announced, which drew a hard stare from his boss. "I say that with all due respect, of course."

Gabriel held the look for a moment, and just as he was about to turn away, Anael nearly jumped out of his skin.

"Holy mother!"

The genuine shock reeling from Anael's face and body caused Gabriel to jump.

"What? What is it?" he cried. These were the first words he had uttered since Lucifer had spoken his final decree that fateful night in the Underworld. How long ago was that? His voice was dry, and his lips felt chapped.

"The thread coming out of you," Anael gasped, "I've never seen anything like it."

"Thread?"

"More like a rope in your case. Glowing and glittering in more shades of purple than I ever thought existed… It's beautiful… no, it's exquisite."

Gabriel racked his brain, trying to understand what Anael was talking about. Something echoed from his pre-heart existence. Anael. Angel of Love and Relationships. His gift is to see the connections between people that others cannot. Right. Threads of light that indicate who's mated to whom; who is fated to whom; who loves whom.

Fate. Love. *Mate*.

Fuck all that, Gabriel thought and snorted his disapproval.

"You could strangle a hippo with what you've got pulsing out of you, Sir," Anael commented.

Normally Gabriel would have retorted with something like 'that's what *he* said,' but he was *not* in the mood.

"Yes? Tell me, then, who's on the other end of it?"

He watched as Anael looked away in respectful refusal. "It is not for me to say, Lord Gabriel. I cannot disclose…"

"You can if I order you to," Gabriel insisted. "Or have you forgotten who you work for?"

"I haven't, sir," Anael said, the look of alarm at hearing Gabriel speaking so out of character spread like fire across his face. "I work for all beings. Including he who is on the other end of this tether."

Gabriel nodded. To say he was cranky and hurting was an understatement, yes. And perhaps he was even behaving like a class-A asshole, but no matter the pain he was in, he wasn't about to force one of his own precious beings to violate a sacred law. Not today anyway.

"Tell you what, how about we meet in the middle. If I guess the name, don't say anything. You won't be breaking any rules that way."

"Well, technically, that's true, but-"

"Achilles?"

"The Greek demi-god?" Anael blinked in shock. "No, no, not him. Apparently, a beautiful-"

"Rasputin?"

"What? Of course not. Mind you, I've heard he was hung like a-"

"Rumpelstiltskin?"

"Ha!" Anael said. "Good one, boss."

Gabriel was firing the names rapidly to

throw Anael off his game.

"Lucifer?"

It worked. He watched Anael's reaction with furious intensity, and the momentary flash in his eyes confirmed what Gabriel already knew.

"I…" Anael stumbled for a moment, looking for a way out of his trap. "I can't say."

"You can neither confirm nor deny," Gabriel pressed. "I get it. Just wanted to know if the bond was still intact or not. You've never seen it before because I had become an expert at keeping it hidden away. Yes, even from you, Anael, no need to be offended."

"Your privacy is of the utmost…"

"I meant no disrespect, of course. I buried it away long before you were even around. It was better that way."

Anael shuffled his feet and cleared his throat. "Unfortunately, I can't say one way or the other, my liege. All I can tell you is that the thread - rope - chain - whatever we should call it, that I can see coming from you is the most substantial I've ever seen and it leads to the Underworld."

"That's all you can see?" Gabriel pressed.

"That's all I can *say*," Anael replied.

The Archangel nodded briskly in response and straightened the cushions on his white leather sofa. He'd been sleeping there the past fortnight - day and night - and it showed. The pizza boxes and beer cans were merely props, but that was real.

"Thank you for your visit, Anael," Gabriel said somewhat too officially. "It has been most… enlightening." He turned away and crossed to his desk, sat down, and began to review whatever file had been sitting there from before. He didn't look back up to Anael but listened for the angel's departure, which followed soon after. The second the door closed, Gabriel threw the file aside and put himself back in the all too familiar head in hands position.

So, our connection remains, Gabriel thought. *You may be able to banish me from your sight and forbid me entrance to your world, but as far as my heart is concerned, you're still my one and only. Anael's little visit has just proved that my attachment to you is not only still strong, but the most exquisite the Angel of Love has ever seen. But is there a similar thread - rope, chain - coming from you to me? Or have you sliced it to pieces like you did my soul? Was there ever a connection between us? Or has this been one-sided all along?*

Another double-edged sword to balance upon. In part, the news helped Gabriel to feel better, his mood lighter. He still felt the pain of rejection - but he also understood that much of his heartache was actually separation sickness from his mate, Lucifer. Misery may love company, and Gabriel wouldn't wish his feelings on his worst enemy, but he took comfort in the knowledge that Lucifer was probably feeling as badly as he did. Was it wrong for him to hope the pain wasn't just one-sided?

If only he could reach out and offer some comfort to him. Some flowers? A bottle of single malt? A small missive written on parchment with the words 'thinking of you'? So little would go so far towards buoying the both of them up.

But Lucifer has closed that window, too, banishing anything from Gabriel from his realm.

"Dammit!" Gabriel shouted as he slammed his fist into the table. The eruption immediately brought a half dozen staff clambering to his door, asking if he was alright and what he needed to be done.

"I'm fine," Gabriel forced a calm he didn't feel. "All is good. Sorry for the disruption."

They all stood there, seeing that he was clearly *not* fine and that all was clearly *not* good.

"Please, get back to what you all were doing. I'm sure it's very important work. Much more important than pandering over my ravings."

Some nods, some murmuring, but one by one, the team dispersed.

Gabriel was alone again, feeling the solitude pressing down on him from all sides, it felt almost oppressive. He looked out the vast windows on the endless blue of creation and was shocked to find himself replaying a memory:

Everyone was gathered in the celestial amphitheater. All the angels, each more beautiful than the next, stood, sat, and lounged in the natural setting. Some were eating grapes; others were sipping nectar. Most everyone was curious about the announcement they had been gathered together to hear.

Gabriel and Lucifer stood side by side. Though they weren't bound by those names or what they implied in that time, in the sweetest of memories, the two of them were inseparable. They ate together, massaged one another, and wandered the endless universe hand in hand. While such exclusive attraction was not forbidden, it was somewhat of an anomaly. All the angels were considered equal, and such couplings out of the group were contrary to the boundaries and definitions of who they were.

The two of them did their best to keep up appearances, spending time with everyone else in an effort to keep the peace. How absurd, Gabriel thought in hindsight, since peace was all there was. Peace, bliss, and eternal indulgence.

The memory continued. Gabriel couldn't believe the pictures flashing through his mind; it was like he had found an old super eight film reel in a cardboard box and was suddenly watching a portion of his life previously lost forever. And the memory wasn't finished.

The crowd of angels went silent when the voice of the Master rang out over the amphitheater.

"My precious children," the voice began. Even during that period, the being behind the voice had never been seen. They were always and only just an audience to Head Office, never spectators. The fact that Gabriel became the right hand for what was only ever a voice, to begin with, spoke highly of his standing after the fall...

The fall! What an expression! It was never intended as a step-down. At least that was the impression that was made during the announcement so long ago.

"I have been laboring at a most remarkable task," the Master continued, "and at last, at long last, I am able to share the fruits of my labor with all of you. It is my hope and wish that all is received in the spirit in which it is being offered: with love, generosity, and hope."

There was a pause in the announcement. Every breath was held, every muscle tensed, every toe bearing the full weight of every beautiful body.

Ripe with anticipation every angel sat pensive, waiting for the voice to continue.

"I have created a new being to join us in our happiness and bliss, I call it: man! He has been fashioned with each of you in mind. My attempts at his beauty speak more to my inability to copy your form, but I hope you will agree I have come close. If this new being was exactly like you, then he wouldn't be new at all, would he? I beseech you, do not see his differences as a reduction or something 'less' than you. Simply a variation."

At that moment, everyone's eyes were opened to seeing the creation just described to them.

Gabriel's first impression of Man was not dissimilar to everyone else's at that time. He was smitten with their innocence and fragility, the way one would react upon seeing a puppy or kitten. Pets, were they? Was that the original intention?

The collective sighs and coos, the murmurings of 'aww' and smiles all around, told Gabriel and Lucifer that everyone was having the same reaction. He felt a hand wrap itself around his. He looked over to his favored angel.

Lucifer looked positively broken as if he had just been cheated on by the love of his life. His eyes, always so full of glorious light, were now glassy and filled with moisture. There had been no cause for tears ever before, so Gabriel didn't quite know what the water in Lucifer's eyes was at the time.

"You know what this means, don't you?"

Gabriel smiled and shook his head. "What?"

"We are no longer alone. Everything will change from this moment onward. Mark my words."

Now that Gabriel was alone, more alone than he had ever been in his life. As much as he tried to refute it in the original moment, one thing was clear: Lucifer saw the writing on the wall long before anyone else had. Would hindsight have made Gabriel's decisions back then any different? If only he could remember what his choices had been and at the time and at least then he would've known how he ended up suffering alone.

Chapter Two

"Where the fuck is Haures?"

Lucifer was yelling at Carmine from the open door of his office. His secretary, accustomed to being yelled at by every demon in the Underworld, had never been spoken to by his boss that way.

"I've sent him your request, my Lord," Carmine calmly replied, "but it has only been two minutes. I'm sure he'll be along as soon as he's able."

"*Able*? If he's not fucking here before I take my next breath, he'll find himself entirely *disabled*."

Lucifer saw Carmine smile diplomatically as he slammed his office door shut.

He was irritable. More so than usual. More so than ever before, if he was totally honest with himself and why not be totally honest? He had nothing left to lose. Ever since the ghost of an ancient memory had been belched up after he recovered from the coma, Lucifer had lost the only friend he ever truly had. What else was there for him to lose?

Unfortunately, the memory in question was incomplete and fuzzy at best. And that's why he had summoned Haures. That slippery little demon was the grandmaster at finding the truth, at seeking the answers to all things past, present, and future. Lucifer was clinging to the hope that Haures' powers extended to the deep, *pre-past* past. The time before Time.

He could recall vivid images of the blissful state he existed in with Gabriel and the others. And he could recollect the earliest memories of his existence immediately after the Fall. The early days of his banishment, the founding of the Underworld, and how he built it up from nothing more than necessity and ideation. But the transition from one state to the other? That memory was patchy as the netherworld, and it was that particular memory edged in a feeling of betrayal that had caused him to cast out his only friend.

Lucifer knew there was something painful in the middle of it all, far beyond the pain of being thrown out on his ass by the Master. And that something had Gabriel's fingerprints all over it. He just wished he knew what it was.

He went over once again the birth of that thought, allowing his mind to ruminate in the blank space where the feeling alluded to the memory, willing answers to come.

It all began here, in his office. He had just woken from what felt like a nap - a fucking endless nap - suffering from a hangover unprecedented in its severity. Malphas was promptly apprehended and hauled off to the pits, and Gabriel - sweet, patient Gabriel - was at Lucifer's side, nursing him back to health.

One moment he felt like kissing Gabriel, and the next, he wanted to kill him. Just like that. It was as if a flicker of doubt had been stealthily floating in the non-air-conditioned office, and he inhaled it like an airborne virus. One breath, and his life was changed. He looked at Gabriel and saw him differently. The trust was gone. The love was lost. The desire curdled like sour milk.

It was then that Lucifer suspected there had been a second betrayal, worse than anything in the history of all treasons, worse even than his own, but he couldn't say precisely what it was. Finally, however, the feeling, the agony of it all, came back with such force that he felt the horror of that moment all over again.

He remembered the words Gabriel had spoken: *Let it go. Move on.* He also recalled that those words were like a knife in his flesh but could not for the life of him piece together what he was asked *to* let go of or *from what* he had been invited to move on from.

Where the fuck was Haures?

If his truth-whispering demon could go back that far and penetrate the moment it all fell apart, then Lucifer might be able to feel some peace. *Maybe*. At the moment, all he felt was a titanic headache, slight nausea, and a cantankerousness to rival Vlad the Impaler.

If he was wrong, and Gabriel was not the betrayer Lucifer had accused him of being, then he would welcome the Archangel back into his life with open arms. If he was right, and Gabriel did stab him in the back, metaphorically speaking, of course, then he would ache on a colossal level. However, he would be justified in his suffering and so, in the best of all possible worlds, move through it as swiftly as possible. Well, that was the plan anyway.

But this… this state of existence based solely on a feeling, a hunch, a fragmented, unreliable memory, was unsustainable, and it hurt like a fucking bitch. He didn't know what was worse, the not knowing or the feeling that Gabriel had betrayed him in the first place.

Lucifer poured himself a drink. He distracted himself by curating a new selection of whiskeys and spirits for his office after the thorough cleansing that happened under Malphas' rule. Once the proud owner of an extensive collection, Lucifer doubled down on ensuring only the finest liquors would fill the gaps on his shelves.

"Shit!" Taking in a mouthful of nineteen twenty-six Macallan should have been like a taste of heaven. Lucifer swished it around, pushing and pulling the golden elixir with his tongue before swallowing. But he couldn't fucking taste it. He had lost all pleasure he'd had in his world the day he told Gabriel to leave, and all that remained was... nothingness.

He ran to the door to bark once more at Carmine. As soon as he flung it open, he was caught unawares by the figure standing on the other side, a hand raised in a pose of pre-knock surprise.

"You called, my Lord?"

"Haures," Lucifer bellowed as he threw his arms around the demon, buried his face in the well-developed chest that smelled of sandalwood, and proceeded to bluster and blubber in tears and snotty expression. "Thank fuck you're here. I need you. Now!"

Lucifer forcefully pulled the demon in and immediately shut the door.

"You don't look so good," Haures quickly spoke. Lucifer nodded in a noncommittal way and more or less threw Haures to the couch. "Uriel sends his regards."

Lucifer noticed the look of concern on the demon's face. "Uriel, yes, fine."

"We're both very happy, my Lord."

"Great," Lucifer replied with impatience.

"I'm not going to let anything fuck that up."

"Fine," the Prince of Lies bellowed, "but why the fuck are you telling me this?"

"You said *I need you. Now.* And then threw me to the couch."

"Are you fucking serious, I don't want to put my dick in you. If I thought my ailment could be alleviated by a tight piece of ass, there's no shortage of willing and able participants here for me to choose from. I'd go through them all like a fucking lawnmower, but that is not what I need or why I called you here."

"Phew," Haures exhaled a sigh of relief. "Right. Good. Glad we cleared that up. So, what exactly can I do for you, my Lord?"

Lucifer explained the pain he was feeling and the gap in his memory. He walked Haures through the pre-time existence, telling him enough to provide some context but not enough to make him feel any more vulnerable than he already did. He also told of his earliest memories as the outcast angel, the founding of the Underworld, and his development as the Prince of Darkness.

"Something happened in between those two states," Lucifer continued, "that I can't quite recall. It's like that period is blacked out in my memory. No matter how hard I try, I can't seem to hold onto anything more than a feeling."

Haures nodded all the way through Lucifer's telling. "I hope you don't mind me asking, my Lord," he said, "but if your memory is totally blacked out, then what makes you think there's anything to be recalled during that time?"

"You mean *what I don't know can't possibly be hurting me* kind of thing?"

"More or less," Haures nodded. "Yeah."

"I was out of commission recently," he said.

"Yes. The coma."

"Nice of you to visit, by the way."

"The Underworld was locked down, and mated demons were denied access, my Lord."

"Save your excuses, it is all in the past now. Anyway, when I was roused out of it and face to face with another from that time-before-Time, whatever was stuffed down my memory bank must have shifted, and the plaster that had sealed the hole shut suddenly cracked."

"Cracked?" Haures asked.

"That's how the light gets through, my boy. Try to keep up. But despite being inundated with strange feelings that started coming, a full-on attack of nagging suspicions, and with them some pretty agonizing memories, I just can't put it all together. All I know for certain is it has something to do with Gabriel, he is at the center of this whole damn mess."

"The archangel?" Haures asked. "Uriel's boss?"

"Would you at least try and keep up Haures, yes, *that* Gabriel, the one and only," Lucifer snapped back. His patience was really at an all-time low.

"Look, I know he's not as innocent as his pure white wings would have everyone believe. But do you really think he would go so far as to betray you, from what you have said – which isn't much- about this time before Time, Gabriel had no reason to hurt you, the Master had already cast you out. Although he did conspire with Uriel to kill Botis, remember? And at the risk of destroying one of his own angels."

"Raziel," Lucifer said with a nod. "I'm well aware of Gabriel's recent transgressions. It's his earlier offenses that I'm a little less clear on. Motive or not, this feeling means something, and I need to get to the bottom of it regardless of what I find."

Haures stood up and wandered the floor of Lucifer's office in contemplation. He stopped at the collection of liquor on display.

"Please, help yourself to a snort if you like," Lucifer said.

Haures poured a scotch from the nearby bottle and winced noticeably.

"Tell me, Haures," he asked. "How does it taste?"

"Like diesel fuel," Haures spat. "You don't happen to have a beer, do you?"

"Fucking heathen," Lucifer whispered to himself. "So, can you dig around and tell me what you can find out?"

Haures set down his glass. "I'll be honest with you, boss; I don't know if my reach goes back that far. Pre-man and all. Not to mention my bias."

"Bias?" Lucifer asked. "What fucking bias could you possibly have other than to me?"

"A world without man," he said. "I couldn't imagine a better scenario if I'm totally honest. But please don't tell Uriel."

Lucifer laughed. "You do realize that your angelic mate would not even be here if not for the existence of mankind. Nor would you, for that matter."

"Yeah. It's a paradox," Haures said. "I'll give it my best shot, boss, but no promises. Whatever I find out, I'll report to you directly."

"Work quickly, Haures," Lucifer added, trying hard to keep the desperation out of his voice. "I'm on a bit of a tight schedule here."

The demon nodded and placed his hand on Lucifer's shoulder in empathy. "I think I understand your predicament, my Lord," he said. "It's no secret to any of us that you and Gabriel…" Haures paused.

"Me and Gabriel, what?" Lucifer barked.

"You have some kind of… I dunno… history. Once upon a time, I wouldn't have understood. But now that I'm sharing my life with Uriel, now that I've bonded with him… well, let's just say I wouldn't want to be in your shoes. So, I hope I'm able to help."

Lucifer thanked him and watched as Haures walked out the door. He caught Carmine's eye and was moved to apologize for his behavior earlier but couldn't find the words in time. As soon as he saw Lucifer looking at him, Carmine quickly shifted his focus back down to his desk and did everything he could think of to appear busy.

Lucifer sighed and slowly closed his office door.

Chapter Three

Gabriel resisted the urge to pace up and down his office. Instead, he forced himself to stand as still as a tree, staying focused and centered, while he awaited his emissary.

Both Michael and Raphael had called in to offer help, healing, and consolations, but Gabriel refused to see them. After his pity party with Anael, he had spent some time engaged in what the humans call 'soul searching,' which was long overdue. What he had found as he suffered through the dark nights of the soul was that he really had no one to blame for his awful mess but himself. It was time to consider a proactive approach to attempting to minimize his suffering, if not for himself, then for the angels that looked to him for solace and strength.

In lieu of a workout, Gabriel took himself for a flight around the globe, stretching his muscles and creating the illusion of having built up a sweat. Then he showered, drank a kale smoothie, cleaned both himself and his office, dressed in his finest, most brilliant whites, and meditated for a few dozen hours.

All of this was extraneous on his part since Gabriel was fully capable of adjusting both his physical body and appearance with a mere thought, but there was power and healing behind the process, and it gave him time to think. He had finally emerged out the other side of his suffering, and while he still held the pain close to his heart, Gabriel was able to find his way out the other side, for now at least.

He summoned Raziel. The Angel of Secrets was Gabriel's best hope for finding out the hidden truths of the deep long-forgotten past with the goal of revealing – once and for all - what had led Lucifer to believe he had been betrayed by more than just the Master and to uncover the truth behind what happened or didn't happen.

"My Lord?" Raziel said upon arrival. Gabriel could see the reaction in Raziel's eyes and knew immediately that he had made the right choice.

"Welcome, dear Raziel. I am in need of your particular gifts."

Gabriel gestured for the angel to sit down, which Raziel did, without taking his eyes off his boss.

"May I say, my Lord," Raziel began,

"you look amazing. Not at all what I was expecting, to be perfectly honest."

"Oh? And what were you expecting, may I ask?"

Raziel stuttered and stumbled through his reply. "Oh, well… some who have come to see you… you know how people talk… I'm sure they were all exaggerating… for effect, you know."

"And I assure you that they were most likely underplaying my state. I struggled my way through a rough patch there for a bit but managed to pull myself out the other side. None of us are immune to the slings and arrows of outrageous fortune. Especially those fortunes that pertain to matters of the heart. Wouldn't you agree?"

"Totally," Raziel nodded.

Gabriel loved the fact that he was exuding not only confidence but magnetism. He had not thought much about how he appeared to others, not in that aspect, of course. But he knew that in order to regain Lucifer's trust and devotion, appearing to be irresistible in all the right ways would be a great help.

"I have an assignment for you," Gabriel began as he sat on the edge of the coffee table, ensuring a higher status over Raziel, who was sunk into the soft leather of the sofa. "I want you to uncover a secret from the past."

"That is the reason for my existence," Raziel said. "What period of time do you need me to search?"

"It won't be as easy as it sounds, I'm afraid. When I say *past*, I mean a past that existed before time itself. A past that wasn't recorded or written down in any way, shape, or form. It is a past that has no survivors to recall other than Lucifer and myself and, of course, the Master, but I doubt you'll get much cooperation from Head Office. Besides, you'd have to go through me to get there, and I'd rather not alert them at this stage."

"Understood, my Lord," Raziel said, but Gabriel could sense the unspoken confusion in his tone. "How far back are we talking then, if we're not able to measure that in time?"

Gabriel smiled. The more he could discuss that time-before-Time, the more - he hoped - the pieces would start to come together. Besides, if he was being honest with himself, he'd been silent about it long enough, and maybe, just maybe, the more he opened up about that long-forgotten part of himself, he would begin to unravel the mysteries that shrouded his apparent betrayal.

"Before everything you know and understand, my dear friend," he began, "Lucifer and I knew each other. There were no words for it then, no list, no choosing one over the other. That was our reality. More of us existed, of course, but he and I became extra close. We lived in a state of eternal bliss and happiness. At least, that's how I remember it. What I don't know is…"

Gabriel cleared his throat, finding it hard suddenly to keep speaking.

"… is if you remember it as it was or rather as you wanted it to be," Raziel said.

"Precisely. I knew you'd understand."

"I try, Sir."

Gabriel nodded curtly and continued. "Then mankind was created, or evolved, or came to be… whatever the actual process was, it was unknown to us. What did we care for the activity of Head Office? We were complete unto ourselves and believed it would last forever – a forever with no concept of time. As a cohort of angels, the Master gathered us together to introduce us to the idea of a new being. It seemed innocent enough at the time, and there was no indication that man's existence would impact ours in any way."

Raziel looked at him with skepticism.

"I can see you consider such a thought naive, and you're probably right. But such was the state of our innocence. We had no experience with anything harming or disrupting or even *changing* the way things were. We were just in our existence and in our existence, as we knew it, nothing had changed before. Until man."

Gabriel went silent and allowed the emotion that accompanied his recollection to sting his eyes.

"So, what happened?" Raziel was literally sitting on the edge of his seat.

"Man wasn't immortal – they were born, they aged, they died and in between that time, they procreated. Life became something that could be measured, as the time went past, man began to flourish, to dream, and to question. Something none of us had ever done because those were concepts we didn't understand. Until the day man's existence did impact us, and something was asked of us."

Another pause. Raziel waited patiently, but it was becoming clear that he was holding his breath.

"What were you asked?"

"I need you to understand that up until that moment, nothing had been asked of us before. We lived, we loved, and we bowed before the Master. Not because we were told to, or asked to, or trained to. But because our love for *Him who Provided All* was so great, so all-encompassing, our bodies just did what they did. We bowed before Him and couldn't express our love strongly enough. Then we were asked…" Gabriel took a deep breath – the next part was so hard. "We were asked to bow before man."

Closing his eyes Gabriel let the tsunami of feeling flood his entire being. He remembered the confusion, the shock, the chaos that such a request unleashed in him. He assumed it must have manifested the same in all the others, but the only one he dared think about was standing beside him at the time.

"I didn't know what to say or how to react," Gabriel continued. "There was no precedence for it. Suddenly all that we had ever known, what we considered our eternal existence, was being called into question. We were being asked to bow to another. We were suddenly thrust from all being *One* to seeing ourselves as *separate* from the Master. We knew we were, I guess, but it never registered on a visceral level, and now all at once, it did. Here was a simple request that served only to shock us into seeing things as they truly were."

"Could you have refused the request?" Raziel asked.

Gabriel smiled a bittersweet grin and began to nod slowly.

"Accepting, refusing… these were not actions we were accustomed to performing. Nobody questioned or challenged the Master before because there was no cause. Now suddenly, there was, and I could see everyone had felt what I had felt, and then almost immediately, the tension seeped out of their faces, and they gave themselves over to simple acquiescence. All but one."

"Lucifer," Raziel said.

Gabriel sucked in his lower lip and tried to nod, but he ended up shuddering and shaking as a tiny squeak of a sob erupted from a place he hadn't tapped for so very long.

"He was instantly defiant. While the rest of us were already slipping back to the status quo, not even considering the upheaval that would eventually bring about the end to that status quo, he was the only one who spoke honestly. Truthfully everyone believes it was due to Lucifer's pride, his ego, and his 'evil' nature that brought about his fall, but they're all wrong. I knew him. I *know* him. It was love. His love for the Master was so great, so true, he could not see the request as anything but a betrayal. Lucifer would not bow before anyone else."

Gabriel rubbed his eyes and tried to pull himself together.

"He hasn't changed in that way," he said, "not one bit. His love is still so strong, his devotion is completely and utterly unshaken by the events of his banishment." He sighed again and spread his arms in a gesture of helplessness. "I'm still in awe of him. I'm still so much less than him. I don't know how to…"

After a number of minutes, maybe

hours, of Gabriel navigating his feelings and memories, he turned to Raziel.

"There's a piece to all of this that's missing. Lucifer knows something, remembers a piece of something that I cannot access. I need you to uncover the secret of what that is, Raziel, and quickly. Despite appearances, I am eroding inside at an alarming rate. I can't be apart from him like this. Nor can he from me, I suspect. We've played these roles long enough, and everything is coming to a head."

"Gabriel, I-"

"Go back, somehow, and find out what's being hidden away from me. I've been successful in rebuilding my memories up to a certain point and then again after. But there's a section that I can't recall, no matter how hard I try, as though a piece of my history has been carved out and the wound stitched masterfully closed."

Gabriel shook his head. "It was like a dream, realizing you had no recollection of how you got to where you were. There's total blankness, nothing but this awful feeling eating away at me, and obviously at Lucifer too. I need to know if I have truly violated something or not. If I have, then I will gracefully accept the consequences of my actions. I will let go, after all this time, I will let go of my love for him, or have it removed, or whatever needs to be done."

"Sir?"

"But if I *haven't* breached our trust, haven't dishonored anything, then I will have to find a way for Lucifer to see and hear this truth from someone other than myself. He will need to know that he is recalling a feeling from a memory that doesn't exist. Then, maybe we can move forward, or at very least go back to the way things were… that was enough… mostly."

Raziel stood up and took a deep breath. For the first time in their friendship, he bowed. "I won't let you down, my Lord," he said.

Gabriel watched as the Angel of All Things Hidden and Unknown flew away and turned his eyes back to the window.

He tried to imagine what letting go would possibly look like and knew that it meant nothing less than his ultimate end. Without Lucifer, there would be no more Gabriel. Well, not a version of himself that he would want to inflict upon the world. As much as that thought terrified him, it was nothing compared to living outside of Lucifer's love. Better to cease his existence than to cause the world to live with the pain of his loss.

Chapter Four

Lucifer was pacing through the halls of the Underworld, more nervous than he could remember being in eons. Maybe more than he had ever been in his existence before. As a rule, the Prince of Darkness had very little, if nothing at all, to make him feel nervous. But this thing with Gabriel was damn near eating him alive from the inside and carving deep lines in his face on the outside.

What would Haures uncover? If Gabriel was guilty of betrayal, then would Lucifer be able to let him go entirely? What would that even mean? If Haures discovered that Gabriel was innocent, then what was the niggling sense of being wronged all about? Would he ever be able to have peace about it? Or would it lead to unrest for the rest of his existence?

There were too many questions, and Lucifer needed answers. Normally he would pound back a few glasses of *aqua vita* and bury his doubts in the ass of a willing demon twink, of which there were thousands to choose from. But not this time. Lucifer knew that for the time being, he was stuck in a state of tasteless chastity until the truth was revealed, and he had some form of closure either way.

The irony was almost too much to bear. He had loved Gabriel right from the beginning, before Time had even come into being. But demons and angels had, at the instruction of the Master himself, always been off-limits to each other. Centuries of pining, longing, of wishing things were different had piled up, and Lucifer had become the poster boy for looking for love in all the wrong places. He knew where his love lived, who held his heart, but such love had been totally forbidden until recently.

Then, low and behold, Master Despot himself had changed His mind, and Head Office was actually encouraging mating between the two opposing beings. Not just urging men to date but mandating it, creating a list, pairing angels with demons for a life of eternal bliss. He knew where it was all leading and required no list to tell him that his time with Gabriel was at long last about to bear fruit. Finally, he could live his truth with Gabriel - the time, at long last, had come.

But there was a bloody giant wrecking

ball-sized pea lodged between the mattresses, way, way down, and he couldn't rest in his lover's bed or his until it had been located and extracted.

Life was simply not fair.

How many times had he heard that refrain bubbling out of the lips of every damned soul who entered the Underworld?

Deal with it, he would tell them all.

Now, he understood.

Lucifer began to make his way back to his office. There were still a thousand and one petty tasks to complete like on every other day, both managerial and administrative. Sadly, he found he had no motivation to do any of them.

As he walked the halls, his eyes roamed over his vast domain. Demons were at work, at play, suffering, loving, fucking, and forgetting. Some were alone, others were together, and still, others were in groups of three or four or fifteen. Souls were being supervised, shepherded from spot to spot, separated and sorted. Life was going on as before, but Lucifer took no interest or love or spark from any of it at all.

He was damned to his own personal

hell: the state of being neither in a relationship nor free of it, and the worst part was he couldn't do a fucking thing about it. He was at the mercy of others to do something for him, and such dependency always drove him to madness.

Fucking Malphas. Fucking coma. I wish I had never woken up.

Lucifer had worked himself up into quite a state by the time he finally arrived back at his office.

The first thing he saw as he rounded the corner, sitting on a chair in the lobby beside Carmine's desk, was Haures, who quickly stood and bowed obediently upon Lucifer's arrival.

"How long have you been waiting?" the Lord of the Underworld asked.

"I dunno," Haures replied. "Twenty minutes? Half an hour?"

Lucifer burned a look into Carmine that would have stopped the heart of any mortal.

"Why the fuck didn't you summon me?"

Carmine pursed his lips slowly, the very statue of patience. "Because my Lord, your last words to me when you went on your ambulatory adventure was '*do not disturb me under any circumstances*.' So, I didn't."

"Oh, for fuck's sake. Sometimes you're too good at doing what you're told," Lucifer grumbled, then opened the door for Haures. "Come in."

He followed Haures in, closing the door behind him. His excitement was like a puppy in front of a treat. It was all he could do to not wiggle his whole body with excitement.

"So?" was all he asked.

"I couldn't get through, my liege," Haures said as he flopped down onto the sofa. "It's like there's a force field or something around that whole time, place, past, whatever or wherever or whenever I was. It's hard to explain. But it definitely impenetrable."

Lucifer sat on the coffee table and tried to remain calm.

"Just tell me exactly what happened," he said. "What did you find?"

"Going back that far is no easy task, let me assure you," Haures began. "It requires a heap of focus and energy. Then there's the job of finding what's been covered up, again, not easy."

"How do you discern between what's been covered up and what hasn't?" Lucifer asked. He realized he had no fucking clue how Haures did what he did.

"It's a sense," Haures said, "an awareness if you like. There's energy emanating either from something or someone, so I follow that using instinct and check it out. Almost as if I am looking for the stone that seems to have been missed, and I turn it over to see what's underneath."

"Ok. So…?"

"So, there are hundreds of souls going back that far. Thousands, in fact, everyone's just milling around. I managed to blend with the crowd by hovering in close proximity to the souls, trying to get a sense of where to go next. We were all standing on the shore of some lake or ocean or river - I can't say which - but a body of water for sure. It doesn't go on forever, but close. We can all sense something, someplace, on the other side, but none of us can get across it."

"Isn't there a ferry or boat or fucking canoe there? I thought there was a ferryman."

"You're thinking of Charon, on the river Styx, which leads to Hades."

Lucifer closed his eyes in embarrassment. *Of course.* He was losing it.

"So, you discovered nothing?" he finally asked.

"I did find one thing of interest," Haures said with half a smile.

Lucifer perked up immediately. "Oh?"

"Raziel was there," he said.

"Raziel?" Lucifer looked off in thought. "What was he doing there?"

"Poking around like me."

"You're sure it was him?"

Haures laughed. "Dead to rights, I'm sure. But, trust me, a gorgeous angel of his stature stands out in a crowd, despite his best efforts to not be seen or noticed."

Lucifer raised an eyebrow.

"Don't worry, he didn't see me," Haures assured him.

Lucifer stood up and crossed over to his desk.

"Gabriel must have sent him," Haures

said. "Any idea why?"

Lucifer shrugged. "Same reason I sent you, I guess. To find out the truth."

"Or to cover it up," Haures suggested.

Lucifer felt ice water suddenly flowing through his veins. Would Gabriel do such a thing? Send his angel of secrets back to cover up the greatest mystery in the history of their existence?

"He wouldn't do that," Lucifer said, trying to reassure himself as much as Haures.

"What makes you so sure?"

"I know him," Lucifer said.

"With all due respect, boss," Haures began, "have you considered that you've given him far too much credit for being pure and innocent all these years? Just because he's an angel doesn't mean he's angelic, if you know what I mean."

Lucifer felt anger rise in him. Despite evidence to the contrary, he still felt protective of Gabriel and would not tolerate anyone casting aspersions on him.

"Watch your tongue," he snapped.

Haures lifted his hands, palms forward,

in a gesture of innocence. "I'm not saying he's guilty or innocent. Just playing advocate for… well, *you*. I worry about you, my Lord."

"You don't need to worry about me, Haures," Lucifer said, dismissing the sentiment.

"Maybe you let your better nature cloud your judgment, that's all."

Lucifer nodded, but his mind was reeling.

"All I'm saying is what I saw. Raziel was there, trying not to be seen. If everything was on the up and up with Gabriel, why was his angel there incognito?"

Lucifer considered Haures' words. He had no answer.

"I know you're disappointed that I wasn't able to access what you wanted," Haures said, "but you can take comfort in the fact that Gabriel's emissary wasn't able to access it either. He was just as barred from penetrating that deep past as I was."

"Yes, yes…" Lucifer mumbled in reply. His mind was now elsewhere.

"Head Office is keeping that time and

place under lock and seal from both demons and angels. Something big is being hidden away, that's for damn sure."

Lucifer nodded wordlessly, and Haures took it as his cue to leave.

The door closed, and the sound echoed around the office. Lucifer held himself up on his desk with both arms for what felt like hours. He wasn't just lost in thought this time, he was lost in the feeling, seeking for the lost memories and, of course, wondering why they were lost to begin with… Why the mystery? What was being hidden, and why?

He didn't want to believe that Gabriel would go so far as to try and cover up the truth. It seemed too out of character for him. If Lucifer was honest with himself, it appeared, more like something a demon would do, like something he himself would do.

Fuck, fuck, fuck!

He was tormented with conflict. Haures was his one and only hope to find out if Gabriel was guiltless or culpable. Now there was no way of knowing. Even if he could ask the archangel, face to face, how could Lucifer believe him? Besides, he'd banished Gabriel. *Out of my sight*, he said. To go crawling back now and to ask if Gabriel was telling the truth or not would be a sign of weakness that Lucifer would never live down.

He had his reputation to consider, after all.

Fuck, fuck, double fuck!

He was in a mess, no question. Walking chaos brought on by that elusive, contradictory, deceptive four-letter word: *love.* What happened to rainbows and butterflies, beer, and brisket, fornicating and desire. *This just plain fucking sucks!*

If only he were a beast, Lucifer wouldn't be clouded by imagination, dreaming, storytelling, and love. If a being was a beast, they lived, ate, fucked, passed on genes, and died. Life was simple, with no complex emotions.

Do monkeys not have fun? Do dogs not express joy? Even a simple house cat - the most self-absorbed mammal on the face of the earth always seems to be blissfully content in its emotional ignorance.

It's come to this, has it? Envious of a domesticated feline!

Lucifer slapped himself across the face. Then again. And again.

Snap out of it, you idiot!

Lucifer was going mad. He had to be. He hadn't felt so untethered or unsure before. Ever. Well, not since…

Son of a bitch!

He suddenly stiffened in a moment of crystallization.

Of course!

The feelings of confusion and pain were not entirely unfamiliar. It had been a long, long time ago, of course, but Lucifer had been down that muddy rabbit hole before.

He recalled his fall from grace, the banishment, his glorious Master throwing him out of paradise. Yes, yes, yes. Lucifer felt the same then - the exact same emotions and confusion then. And all due to the short but potent, four-letter word: love.

His love for the Master caused him such grief. Now his passion for Gabriel – even greater, Lucifer was now forced to admit, than his love for the Master - was reducing him to the same state of idiocy.

A question was born in the deep recess of his soul and bubbled up to the surface, like a single cell organism breathing oxygen for the first time.

Do I regret it?

Lucifer had never asked himself that before. If he could go back in time and do as he had been asked – to bow before man as requested by the Master…

… if his love had been reduced by a tenth of a percent, his love for his maker…

… would he? Would he do it all differently, knowing what he knew now?

All those centuries, the endless recruitment and training of demons. The legions of hell, its princes, and lords. The infinite amount of souls being shepherded through the Underworld, the ongoing torment, and torture for their failed attempts to achieve grace above.

The countless millennia watching Gabriel from afar, longing, suffering, wanting nothing more than to be with him.

What if he had bowed? What if he did what all the others did at that moment?

His pantomime of pain, the charade of grief… it would all be gone, it never would have existed in the first place.

Imagine no fall, imagine no heaven, no hell below us. Above us, only the sky.

Fuck! Now a pop song was running through his mind. It was a temporary distraction, though. Lucifer allowed his mind to wander through a set of scenarios he had never once previously considered. And the brief insight into the past was helpful.

Compassion and empathy found a way, as they always do.

Is this what Gabriel is feeling now?

Chapter Five

"What do you mean you can't get in?" Gabriel asked in a most exasperated tone. Raziel's report was not what he'd expected.

"I mean, it's restricted, blocked, locked up. I can't get in, and nor can anyone else, it seems."

Gabriel pinched the corners of his eyes together, as he typically did when his stress levels were at an all-time high. *Blocked* was not the word he wanted to hear. Raziel had been his last chance. If Raziel couldn't uncover the secrets that were hidden away, then who could? Haures, maybe, but he worked exclusively for Lucifer and things being what they were, Haures wouldn't assist. Gabriel considered briefly going through Uriel. Uriel owed him, owed him big, and the two had enough bad business between them... what was one more request?

No. He couldn't ask that of Uriel. Besides, Haures was loyal to both his mate and his boss. There was no way to slice it that created any loyalty to Gabriel.

"Head Office must have it sealed off

entirely, I should have known."

But why? What was the Master doing, keeping a specific episode - if such an episode even existed - hidden away from Gabriel? It was *his* life, wasn't it? Didn't he have full and unfettered access to his own life, warts and all? It was not like Head Office to bury something away. Unless it implicated them somehow, but how could it? The memories Gabriel was looking for were clearly related to himself and Lucifer and Lucifer's opposition to the Master's decree. What could be more damaging than that? The entire realm of creation knew of Lucifer's actions of defiance and the Master's punishment, so why couldn't he see what those actions had done in his relationship with Lucifer.

Gabriel dropped himself down onto the sofa like a weighted blanket.

"I'm sorry, my Lord," Raziel said, "I've failed you."

"You haven't failed anything, my dear angel. Forces greater than you and I are at work here. I sent you on an impossible mission, thinking it was a simple errand. It is I who should apologize to you. Thank you for trying."

"Of course, my Lord."

"Tell me… what was it like? Maybe your description will help jog my memory."

Raziel described the earthy smell as soil that had recently been tilled. Fig trees grew in abundance, and the milling souls sustained themselves on the endless supply of fruit that grew upon their branches.

"There was the sound of water," Raziel went on, "and I made my way slowly to where it was coming from. A river, I suspected, as it was moving, but I've never seen a river quite like that. It appeared as expansive as an ocean. It seemed endless. Beyond that, I could see the light was fading as if watching a sunset. I knew what I was looking for was on the other side of that river somehow, but I wasn't able to step in it, let alone venture across."

Gabriel savored Raziel's description of the place, relishing each detail. Unfortunately, nothing sounded remotely familiar, but it seemed a lovely spot all the same.

"One more thing," Raziel added. "Haures was there."

Gabriel's eyebrows lifted. It was too early to say whether it was in hope or surprise, but they lifted up, and with them, light filled his eyes.

"Haures? Did you speak with him?"

"No. It looked like he didn't want to be seen, so I respected that. But he was poking around just as I was."

"And did he see you?"

"Not a chance. There was a large crowd of souls gathered at the border, so I blended in."

Gabriel's head tilted at the information of a large crowd of souls. "How many?"

"Hundreds, I'd say. Maybe a thousand. It seems Haures and I aren't the only ones curious about the ancient past. All of them looked like they had been there forever and a day. Who were they?"

Gabriel shook his head. "Hard to say. Things didn't happen smoothly in the beginning, and soul transitioning took a while to master. Lucifer was establishing his realm, and Head Office was establishing ours. It's entirely possible that some may have fallen through the cracks, as it were."

"Shame. They deserve to rest as much as anybody else."

Gabriel nodded. "Agreed. I'll bring it up with Head Office."

He said that without fully thinking through the ramifications. "Of course, they'll want to know why I had you poking around there, which will open a can of celestial worms I'd rather they didn't know about just yet."

He was talking more to himself than to Raziel, so he was a bit surprised when he looked up and saw the expression of concern on the angel's face.

"I'll take care of it," he assured Raziel. "They will find rest. The bigger question has to do with Haures. What was *he* doing there? Clearly sent by his boss, but to what end?"

Raziel stifled a laugh. "A demon sent by Lucifer? Obviously up to no good. Whatever secret or truth you sent me to uncover may be a threat to him. Maybe Haures was there to destroy it, wipe it out altogether?"

Gabriel mulled the thought around for about ten seconds, then spat it out. "No. The threat is clearly on me, not him. Perhaps Lucifer sent Haures there because he's uncertain of his own motivations? His hunch is that I betrayed him, but it's only a hunch. He has no clear memory of it. Maybe Haures was there so that Lucifer could prove himself wrong. Maybe he's trying to clear my name as much as I am."

Raziel's eyes widened, and he swallowed as slowly and as quietly as he could. "Uhhh… sure. I guess. Anything's possible."

"You seem skeptical."

Raziel appeared to be shaking his head and nodding all at the same time. "Forgive me, Gabriel, but I *am* skeptical of Lucifer. He's the Prince of Darkness, the Lord of Lies. He was outcast by the Master for refusing to follow a commandment. He's not renowned for his compassion or generosity. He is, however, known far and wide to be obstinate, insubordinate, and defiant. Why do you insist, over and over again, upon giving him the benefit of the doubt?"

"Because I love him."

The simplicity of Gabriel's words, carried by that deep and authoritative voice, must have hit Raziel like a fist.

"Now, either my love for him has blinded me to his true nature, which I fully admit is possible. Or…"

"Or…?"

"Or I see his true nature in ways no one else can, and that is why I love him as I do. Either way, I don't share your skepticism, but I appreciate that you feel safe enough to confess it to me. That's why I trust you with all of this."

Raziel nodded in humble acknowledgment of Gabriel's words. "So now what?" he asked.

Gabriel ran his hands through his hair and down over his face. "I need you to arrange a meeting."

"Easy peasy, with whom?"

"Lucifer."

"Sir?"

"He and I both want the same thing. To understand the truth of what happened so long ago. Neither of us is able to access that information on our own. So, we must discuss the possibility of how to access the truth, if that's impossible, or how to move on with never knowing it. Either way, I can't continue living like this, and I'm willing to bet he can't either."

"He doesn't trust you right now. He banished you from his sight. What makes you think he'll even agree to a meeting?"

Gabriel spread his arms wide. "He has just as much to lose as I do, living like this. We can't do our jobs with any efficacy. If he loves me as I suspect, he does - as I love him - he'll want to do what's best."

Raziel stood up.

"Ok. I'll arrange it. But you should have Michael there with you, just to be safe."

"No. Michael was with him during the lowest point of his existence. He might associate Michael with his coma and the dredging up of this half memory in the first place. No, that won't do at all."

"I'm sorry, but I must insist."

Gabriel sighed. He knew Raziel was right and was only doing his job. He also knew it would be futile to fight Raziel about it. His angels were as loyal to their jobs, as he usually was to his.

"Very well. But please tell him to be discreet, more than discreet - invisible."

Raziel nodded affirmatively.

"You can be there," Gabriel added. "I'll assume he'll have Haures there with him, but at some point, I'm willing to bet we'll want some privacy. So please choose someplace neutral, where neither of us will appear to be too much out of our element."

"Understood."

Raziel's wings emerged as he made his way to the door. Gabriel watched him through the window, descending easily down through the clouds to pay a visit to Lucifer.

How easy he makes it look, Gabriel thought with a tinge of envy. He promised himself, whatever the outcome, to never take love - or those he loved - for granted again.

Chapter Six

Club AZ was busier than ever before. Dancers commanded both the floor and the stage. A team of bartenders was working non-stop behind the long oak bar, pulling pints of ale and mixing cocktails with precision and efficiency. Bouncers managed the long line of revelers seeking to gain entrance with only the occasional incident, but that was simply part and parcel of the club scene, and it was rare that someone got hurt – too severely.

Lucifer sat and took it all in. He was drinking a soda and lime – there wasn't any point in drinking anything else - and awaited Raziel.

Haures was in the bar with him but seated a few tables away. He was enjoying his pint of pale ale, visiting with Zagan. Zagan co-owned the place with his angel mate Anael, who was also there, enjoying himself on the dance floor.

"He looks good, wouldn't you say?"

Lucifer turned his head away from Zagan towards the voice at his table.

"Happy."

"Raziel," Lucifer said with a somewhat

forced smile. "How nice to see you again. Please, have a seat."

The angel sat down across from Lucifer and laced his fingers together on the table.

"How's the cab business, by the way?" Lucifer asked. "Keeping you busy, I hope?"

"Oh, you know…" Raziel smiled, "everyone needs help getting where they need to go, at some point or another."

Lucifer nodded and sipped his drink. "And Botis? Haven't seen him for ages. He's well? You're both happy?"

"Blissful," Raziel said, then paused with a smile.

"What?" The word rippled through Lucifer like a lightning bolt,

"You never struck me as one who engaged in small talk," Raziel said, pulling Lucifer back to the room. "You're not nervous, I hope?"

Lucifer forced a casual laugh. He wasn't nervous, but his psyche resembled a man on the brink of a trip to a psychiatric facility for a long, pleasant holiday in a padded cell. His nerves were frazzled and shot. He honestly didn't know *what* he was.

"Should I be?"

Raziel lifted and dropped his shoulders in time to the music coming from the dance floor.

Lucifer smiled. He knew damn well that he was in love. The realization came with doubt and anxiety, but he had to call things what they were. There was no point lying to himself, even if he was trying to hide his feelings from everyone else.

No regrets, no regrets, no regrets.

"Nothing to be nervous about when it comes to Gabriel, is there?" Lucifer asked. Despite being mired in the quicksand of lovesickness, he couldn't help stirring the shit, just a little bit, it was his nature to be quick-witted. "I mean, you'd know, I guess. You were the intended target of a certain plot once upon a time. Gabriel conspired with one of your colleagues to kill you, didn't he?"

"Uriel," Raz replied flatly. "And you know very well who it was."

"Right. The name escaped me for a moment. I've got a lot on my mind, my apologies. So, you tell me, Raziel. Would *you* be nervous about meeting with Gabriel?"

"Damn right I would be if I were you. The possibility of losing the love of my life over selfish, paranoid behavior that I'd regret forevermore would scare the living shit out of me."

Lucifer felt the blood drain out of his cheeks. *The nerve of this little prick.*

"But that's just me," Raziel added with a gentle smile. "I'm sentimental that way."

"Love of my life," Lucifer snorted. "Just because you're getting laid on a regular basis with ballsy Botis doesn't mean we all see the world the same way you do."

"So why bother with all of this," Raziel asked, "if not for love?"

"I have a working relationship with Gabriel," Lucifer replied. "I need to trust him. Loving or not loving has nothing to do with it."

Raziel looked at him as if watching a magician perform an inexplicable routine. "It's amazing that you can lie so effortlessly to me. I'm nothing to you in the grand scheme of things. You can lie to your fellow demons, maybe you can even lie to yourself for an extended period of time. But this I know: lies only push you further away from happiness. If Gabriel is your intended mate, you won't be able to lie to him."

Lucifer let out a mighty belly laugh. Loud enough to turn heads from the pounding dance floor. "You angels are sooooo self-righteous. You think because you don't lie that you're somehow perfect. Light-years above us lowly demons."

"Not at all."

"So, tell me, were you sent to the ancient past by Gabriel?"

"I was," Raziel answered calmly.

"To what end?"

"You'll have to ask the one who sent me," he said. "I cannot share confidential information."

"So where is he, then? Gabriel. I thought you were arranging a meeting for us, not you and I."

"He'll be along when he's ready, I'm sure," Raziel answered. "But while we're waiting, may I ask you something?"

"Fire away," Lucifer snapped back.

"I saw Haures when I was trying to

penetrate the secrets of the past. You sent him?"

Lucifer looked surprised. He turned his face towards where Haures was sitting, already on his third beer, laughing with Zagan. "Fuck it all, yes, I sent him. What is it to you?"

"To what end?"

Lucifer shifted in his seat. He was getting uncomfortable with this. Where was Gabriel?

"Same reason as Gabriel sent you, I imagine, to uncover the truth."

"Uncover it?" Raziel pressed. "Or destroy it?"

Lucifer opened his mouth to respond, but no words came. He hadn't considered the idea of destroying the truth. Is *that* what Gabriel intended?

Oh, fuck! Have I been wrong all this time?

He lowered his face into his hands and pressed his palms against his eyes. Lucifer couldn't remember the last time he wept, and he wasn't about to let this angel see him reduced to tears.

Just keep it together, he told himself. *You're the Lord of the Underworld, for fuck's sake. What the hell's the matter with you?*

No regrets, no regrets, no regrets. He kept repeating it to himself like a mantra.

He felt a hand on his shoulder.

"Everything all right here, my Lord?"

He turned around to find Haures standing there, looking concerned. At his side was Uriel. Across the table, Lucifer saw that Raziel was no longer seated. He stood close by, hand in hand with Botis.

Fuck me, how long was I looking away?

Beside them were Zagan and Anael. Wasn't Anael dancing a few seconds ago?

Lucifer craned his neck around to check out the dance floor. All the bodies there were suspended in time. Arms up, hips out, feet akimbo, frozen in their joy.

The entire bar was a crowded snapshot, save for the bodies around the table. A few tables over were two other couples. Seir was sitting on Raphael's lap, and beside them stood the archangel Michael and his new mate Orobas.

Everyone looked to Lucifer, not with

judgment or malice or anger, but with concern, warmth, even love.

"What the fuck is this?" Lucifer mumbled. "An intervention?"

"We're concerned for you," Botis said. "That's all."

"Look around, my Lord," Zagan said, gesturing to the five couples gathered around, "you're responsible, along with Gabriel, for so much love and joy."

"I'm not in the mood for an episode of *This Is Your Life.*" Lucifer tried to keep calm, but he despised being the center of a show he hadn't orchestrated. *Were they rubbing my nose in their fucking happiness?*

"We wouldn't be together without your help and input," Raziel added. "You pretend to be immune to love, that you can reject your feelings and somehow banish the source of your joy, but you can't. You're as much a part of this as the rest of us."

"One of the orchestrators, in fact," Anael said.

"You've brought balance to the universe after so long," Seir offered.

"And in the process, you've brought

much peace and fulfillment to all of us," Raziel added. "Why deny it for yourself?"

"Because," Lucifer barked. "My one true love betrayed me."

Everyone went silent and still.

"You think you've all suffered so much to be with your mates," he continued, "but what the fuck do you know about sacrifice? About patience? I've been silent for millennia. Longing for the only man I could ever love, and he was forever out of reach. It was forbidden. Can't you see? *Forbidden*. To me. To him. By decree of the one Being who is supposed to be all about love and balance, as you say. I cry foul. I cry bullshit."

"But you don't know for sure if he betrayed you," Haures said. "What if you're wrong?"

"I can't deny what I feel," Lucifer countered. "Something's not right about it all, and until I find out the truth, we don't stand a fucking chance."

"He loves you, Lucifer," Raziel said. "He's loved you since the beginning of time. Even before time began. Are you honestly willing to throw that away on a hunch?"

"No," he shot back. "That's why I sent Haures to verify it. But he couldn't get in. Nor could you, by the sounds of it."

"Head Office has it all sealed off," Raziel said. "Any idea why the Master would do that?"

Lucifer laughed to himself. "The Master," he repeated, then shook his head. "Masterful pain the ass is what He is."

Some looks of shock and alarm crossed the faces of everyone present.

"Don't look so alarmed," Lucifer said, "it's nothing to shit your shorts over. He knows exactly how I feel. I've never pulled any punches with Him before, and I'm not about to start now. If He's sealed it off, He's done so for a reason. I'll be damned if I know what that reason is, but there's a method to His madness. There always is. That old boy has something up his sleeve with this; make no mistake."

"Or He's trying to protect you," Michael said. "Keep you safe."

"From what?" Lucifer shouted. "From having what you all have? Must He punish me for all time because I wouldn't…"

He shut his eyes in painful frustration and tightened his fists. *Fuck*! Lucifer screamed, and his voice echoed throughout the bar.

"I loved Him in ways you cannot even begin to imagine," Lucifer confessed, his voice choking on emotion. "And I would have done anything for Him. Do you understand? Anything. I'll never forget when He asked - that's right, *asked* - that we bow to none before Him. He didn't even need to ask. I would have done it freely. I had been doing it freely all along. And I remember when he demanded - not asked this time but *demanded* - that we now bow to them. *Them*!"

He gestured broadly to the hundreds of bodies on the dance floor, and those gathered around the bar, their faces frozen in time. What were once expressions of innocent fun now looked purely ridiculous.

"He believes I disobeyed him," Lucifer softly spoke, his voice was quieter now, "when, in fact, I was the only one who had the balls *to* obey him. And for that, I'm forever damned to be alone, forbidden to love."

"Is that what you truly believe, my Lord?" Haures asked. "In your secret heart of hearts?"

"Who the fuck knows?" Lucifer retorted. "I haven't got a clue what's in my heart. Have you?"

Haures slowly shook his head.

"Have any of you?"

They all stood still as statues. None could say what was in the heart of another.

"You told me one time that the Master knows who *holds* your heart."

This deep, sonorous voice cut through the sorrow and tension of the room like a razor.

"Do you remember, Luc? Back when all this mating buzz began, you told me then, *The Master already knows who holds my heart.*"

All eyes flew around the bar. A body from the dance floor turned and started walking towards Lucifer's table.

"And you know as well, don't you? Who holds your heart?"

Lucifer's eyes filled with tears. "Yes."

Lucifer turned in his chair and beheld

the object of his affection, his love, his longing. Gabriel spread his arms out.

"I've always been right here for you. Never question that."

Was he inviting me to hug him?

The pull to fly into Gabriel's arms was strong. More potent than any force known to Lucifer. He had to grip the arms of the chair he was sitting in until his knuckles went white to stop himself from flying heart-first into that embrace.

"Thank you, everyone. Please leave us," Gabriel quietly said.

The others turned and walked slowly away as the dancers and revelers came back to life. The music faded back in, and the lights returned to their blinding show.

"Let's get out of here," Gabriel suggested.

Lucifer stood and followed him without protest.

Chapter Seven

Once outside, Gabriel had to slow his walking pace so Lucifer could keep up. His shorter legs were working double-time to match Gabriel's long strides.

"How long were you in there for?" Lucifer asked, trying to catch his breath.

"I was there before you even arrived," Gabriel replied, grateful to have Lucifer behind him so he couldn't see the smile on the archangel's face.

"You'd have made a great demon," Lucifer commented, "with the ability to stay hidden and not be detected like that. You could have caused such mischief and strife."

"What makes you think I haven't caused my fair share?"

It was still early evening, and Gabriel walked towards a playground in a public park. There were a few children playing with their parents nearby, but nobody seemed to mind two grown men walking amidst the slides, swings, and monkey bars.

Gabriel was dressed well, as always, but casually appropriate for the season. Early fall in Seattle was typically on the chilly side, so his light cream-colored pullover and tan linen slacks were sufficient. Not that he felt the cold - or warmth, for that matter. He was impervious to earthly temperatures.

Lucifer, on the other hand, wore his standard traveling outfit: a leather jacket, faded jeans, and motorcycle boots. A blood-red t-shirt was his signature item, and it was perfectly cut to showcase his small but well-developed chest, abs, and arms. He felt every chill, however, and so was trying to zip his jacket up tighter. He pulled the large collar up as high as it would go, causing Gabriel to laugh.

"What's so funny?" the defensive demon asked.

"You look like a pint-sized vampire."

"I'm cold. Sue me."

"Here," Gabriel offered with a subtle wave of his finger.

"Ooooh, that feels good," the Lord of the Underworld said with satisfaction. "What did you do?"

"Regulated your body temperature, so you don't feel the cold," he said. "I want you to be comfortable."

Lucifer nodded in thanks and lowered

his collar. He sat down on the bottom end of a seesaw, his knees bent so that his legs spread out behind him.

"Must be nice," he mumbled.

"What's that?" Gabriel asked.

"To be able to snap your fingers and have whatever you want, whenever you want it."

Gabriel considered Lucifer's words. He rarely thought about his abilities.

"We all have our gifts and tricks," he said, "as you know. Besides, I wouldn't feel too jealous. Even mine has its limitations."

"Like what?"

"Well, I can't move us past this little obstacle very well, can I?" Gabriel said as he lifted his legs on the opposite raised end of the seesaw, drawing the seat down to the earth with his body weight, watching Lucifer rise up the other side. He was looking into Gabe's eyes for the first time since they left the club.

"Do you want to?" the Dark Lord asked.

"More than you could possibly imagine," Gabriel answered without a second's hesitation. "Do you?"

He was surprised - and a little hurt - to see Lucifer shrug. "I don't know, to be honest."

Gabriel pushed gently off the ground with his feet and felt himself lifting into the air.

"Really?" Gabriel's voice stuck in his throat.

"Really... Something happened between us at the beginning of all this, Gabriel, and I don't know if I want to just 'get past' it. I need to understand what it was, why it happened, and then decide what it all means for our future."

"Our future together, or..."

"Well, this is it, I just don't know, and frankly, I find it disturbing that you'd just wave a magic wand and sweep all the unanswered questions under the carpet if you could. For what? So, we can be like the rest of them? Mated and domestic?"

Gabriel had a flash vision of the two of them sharing a life together. Sharing a bed and bodily fluids of all manners and types, traveling, laughing, holding each other close as a new day dawned.

The seesaw lowered him down again, raising Lucifer up.

"Mated doesn't sound so bad, does it?" Gabriel asked, feeling his prick starting to plump up.

Lucifer trembled, ever so slightly, and then straightened his back to hide it. But Gabriel caught it and knew that his demonic counterpart wanted the same thing.

"Gabriel, I know I'm not renowned for my honesty and vulnerability," Lucifer said, "but please believe me when I say that I would love nothing more than to wrap my legs around your beautiful hips and feel you deep inside me for the rest of time. That's all I've ever wanted and all I shall ever want. Nothing else matters."

For the first time in a billion years, Gabriel felt truly ignited. He was ready to take him right here in the playground.

"Except…" Lucifer continued.

Except….????? Those two syllables echoed in Gabriel's ears and blinded him to all the hope as if a star had just exploded in his face.

"Except what?" Gabriel begged. "What could matter more than that? What could matter more than us being together?"

"The truth. I need to know what happened. Don't you think *we* need to know, deserve to know?"

Gabriel hung his head and tried to feel the ground with his feet to dismount. He was surprised to see that he was suspended in the air and doubly surprised to see that Lucifer was in the exact same position. Despite the vast discrepancy in their respective body weights, they were balanced on the seesaw.

"Luc," he whispered. Lucifer, also appearing to be lost in thought, lifted his head.

"Yeah?"

"Look at us. We're perfectly balanced."

Lucifer turned his head around and looked up and down. "What the actual fuck? This is physically impossible."

The two of them bounced their asses up and down but were unable to shift the balance that had been struck.

Suddenly the sky went dark as if a mighty hand had flipped a switch, and the entire surrounds of the playground began to spin. The two remained still, fulcrum-like, while the universe rotated and revolved around them in a hurricane of spectacle that could only be the working of one single entity.

Gabriel looked over to Lucifer, seeing only his silhouette in the shadowy half-light, but it was enough for him to make out the words being formed in the mouth of the Prince of Darkness:

"Fuck me up the-"

Then a blinding light came burning down from above. It was bright and harsh after so much dusk and dark, like the moment when the fluorescents burst on at the club after last call was announced. Gabriel stole a glance at Lucifer and wondered if he himself looked as unflattering in this unforgiving beam as Luc did.

The air rang with the deafening clang of a bell, and both angel and demon alike instinctively pressed their hands to their ears in an attempt to muffle the sound.

"My dear children," a voice thundered through the darkness. "Look at the two of you playing so nicely on your little teeter-totter."

The light shifted from side to side, shining first on Gabriel and then over to

Lucifer. It cast a sharp shadow on the ground of the two of them suspended in equilibrium on the board. Gabriel couldn't help but feel that they were a couple of ants caught under the fiery glare of a barbaric child's magnifying glass.

Lucifer turned his face away from the light.

"Balance," the voice boomed. "This is what it's all about. Good and evil, old and new, Head Office and the Underworld, angels, and demons. You have both worked hard and followed my commands diligently. I am most pleased."

"How fucking delightful," Lucifer whispered. Gabriel heard his sarcasm and hoped that the Master didn't. Or, if so, that He was magnanimous enough to look past it. Likely door number two.

"I have observed everything, watching closely how the two of you would manage your respective teams, and I have to say you've surprised even me, and that takes some doing."

"It has been an honor, Sir," Gabriel said with head bowed.

"Oh, stop kissing his ass, Gabe," Lucifer

shouted. "I can't stomach it anymore. I swear I'll puke right here on this sacred and holy ground if I have to listen to one more word."

Gabriel was frozen with horror. None ever spoke in the presence of the Master this way; it was brazen, even for Lucifer.

"Do you have something you wish to say to me, Lucifer?" the voice rumbled. Gabriel could hear the patience working hard to keep the wrath at bay.

"No, your worship," Lucifer replied with measured diplomacy. Gabriel exhaled a heavy sigh of relief. "I have a *thousand* things to say."

Oh, fuck!

"Please, my child. I'm all ears."

"First of all, you speak as if we're middle management in your grand corporate empire."

That's precisely what we are, you idiot. Gabriel thought it but didn't speak.

"We're not. I speak for Gabriel and myself when I say we Don't. Work. For. You."

Yes, we bloody well do!

"At best, we work *with* you, and at

worst, we're on our own. Most often, it's the worst-case scenario. Don't get me started on the countless occasions where you've conveniently disappeared, just when things with your little pets got out of control."

The Voice was silent. Gabriel was waiting for his heart to start beating again.

"Am I wrong?" Lucifer looked to Gabriel. The archangel opened his mouth only to discover he couldn't find his breath, let alone the words, to reply.

"Proceed," the Voice uttered, over-annunciating the 'd' after the snake of the 'cee' ran its course.

Gabriel was astonished. Not only had the Master NOT smote Lucifer down, but he had also condoned the outburst by asking for more.

And to think the age of miracles had long since passed!

"As for *managing* your request," Lucifer continued, growing bolder now in his delivery - in fact, Gabriel thought he actually appeared taller- "we managed nothing. Two souls - one angel, one demon - found each other and managed themselves through the trials and tribulations of committing to each other. It happened five times over. Nothing to do with us, and - since I've got your undivided attention - nothing to do with you. You wrote a list and dropped it in our laps, nothing more, the rest took care of itself."

Gabriel found himself nodding slightly to Lucifer's reasoning. He wasn't far off.

"You seem to be a fountain of insights, my child," the Voice decreed. "How far you've come."

"Yeah, well, I had a lot of time to ruminate as I lay in a fucking coma fighting for my life and realm. Tell me, was that your doing, oh Mighty one? Did you unleash Malphas on me?" Lucifer looked to Gabriel. "On us?"

Silence.

"I'll take your silence as a 'yes.' Fine, I'm sure you have your reasons, you always do."

"Your point?"

"My point is that everything has somehow led to this: the man I love sitting across from me, within reach, and yet lightyears away, separated by infinite time and space the same as he has been for what feels like eternity."

The light shifted to Gabriel.

"Tell me, child," the voice said to the archangel, "do you feel the same way?"

Gabriel swallowed. He was never one for being direct with the Master, but Lucifer was positively aglow with confidence and vigor. The attraction, the pull to him, was almost unbearable.

"Yes, sir," he heard himself say. "I do. I agree with everything my colleague, my friend," he looked to Lucifer, "my one true love... has said. I stand with him."

Another moment of silence, which Gabriel punctured with a pleading *"Respectfully."*

Lucifer mouthed 'pussy' with a smile and a wink.

"Very well. I have taken on your words - all of them - but shall listen no more."

The light was starting to fade when Lucifer bellowed as loud as thunder:

"Wait! I'm not finished."

The light turned back once more.

"You dare test my patience, child?"

Gabriel was shaking his head now, willing Lucifer to keep his mouth shut.

Don't push it, Luc.

"We need to know what happened," Lucifer yelled. "You must unlock the secrets of the past."

"Must I?"

"Please, my Lord," Gabriel added. "What Lucifer is trying to say is… we hope your benevolence will see fit to… lift the veil, so to speak, and allow our memories to be restored."

A low chuckle rippled across the wind. "We have a poster hanging here in Head Office, do you know what it says?"

Gabriel shook his head while Lucifer awaited a response with his arms crossed over his chest, looking for all the world like an overly petulant toddler.

"Sometimes God will give you exactly what you *want* just to show you it's not what you *need*."

Lucifer rolled his eyes. "Thank you, Mick Jagger. Now, if you're done sharing your bumper sticker collection, can you give us a straight answer to a straight-up question?"

"Please," Gabriel pleaded. "Show me where I went astray."

"Where *we* went astray," Lucifer threw

in, then turned to Gabriel and whispered, "if we're going to fuck ourselves over forevermore, at least let's do it together."

The bright light dimmed lower and lower until it was out completely; the dark sky returned to the golden dusk of before; and the playground equipment repaired to its rightful place as both Lucifer and Gabriel landed with a heavy thud on the ground, each getting their balls rattled against the hard plastic of the seesaw seats.

Three words whispered in the air during the transition back to status quo would have been taken for mere wind by any set of ears save for the two who heard them.

As. You. Wish.

Chapter Eight

Lucifer always considered himself a good sleeper. Despite the stress and strain of the work, he was engaged in - the weight of every human soul that entered the Underworld was on his shoulders, let's be honest - he did not suffer from insomnia. He slept, as they say, like a baby, or considering babies don't sleep very well at all, maybe it is more accurate to say he slept like the peaceful dead – only he could wake up at will.

His dreams were vivid, easily recalled, and just as quickly forgotten if he so chose. Like anyone else, he worked out daytime problems at night while he slept, and the images were extraordinary.

That is why, when Lucifer woke up the day after the intervention, it wasn't the foreign surroundings that first struck him as bizarre, nor the fact that he was entirely naked. There was nothing novel nor alarming about that. But what was weird was that he had no instant recollection of any dreams. Nor could he remember falling asleep; that last thought, idea, or sensation before dropping off evaded him.

Throughout his existence, that experience had only happened twice before. Most recently, prior to slipping into his coma, Lucifer had been unable to recall anything about the final moments preceding *that* experience. The first time, of course, was after he was thrown out of paradise by the Master. He couldn't remember the night before waking up then either; there were huge chunks of time and events he couldn't remember prior to 'then.' Which of course was the reason the intervention was necessary.

Something was covering his face, Lucifer pulled off a coarse fabric in a tasteless grey/shit-brown color - it was a hooded cloak. He held it in his hand, bunched up, as he looked around and blinked himself into consciousness. He was on the ground, which wasn't at all cold or particularly hard. The sun - or what he *assumed* was the sun - was rising in the distance. The air was neither warm nor cool, but something blandly in the middle. Room temperature, despite the fact there were no walls or ceiling or *room* in any direction.

Beside him were others. Other men, all naked as the day they were born. Each one was fast asleep. Everybody was similar, not to mention spectacular in form, but the faces were all covered in the same rough, drab cloak. Was he supposed to put this on? Was it designed to keep him warm in case a storm blew in? Lucifer had no damn idea. It was all incredibly strange.

Where the fuck am I?

Lucifer got to his feet and began to walk around, determined to get a better idea of where the fuck he was. His bare toes made contact with the earth, it felt softer than any surface he had walked on before. The sight of the sleeping bodies continued for as far as he could see. Hundreds, maybe thousands of exquisite men in their birthday suits, slumbering soundlessly and still.

Lucifer noted that nobody snored or moved in their rest. Everyone was lying on their backs, their hands at their sides. Some of the penises, Lucifer couldn't help but notice, were erect or on their way to hardening, but most were flaccid and either lying to one side or simply poking up through their tiny little hoods. White, black, big, small, thick as rolling pins, or thin as cheap cigars. Each was different, but they all had one thing in common - not a single prick was circumcised.

The Lord of the Underworld also noted that everyone lying on the ground was taller than him. That was nothing new in his experience, but for some reason, it bothered him. *Is it morning?*

He stepped gingerly through the sleeping bodies, careful not to disturb anyone until he came to the edge of wherever the fuck he was and found himself standing at the bank of a mighty river.

He knew he had never been here before, but that didn't stop him from feeling that this was all too familiar. That's when it struck him – he was in the place Haures described to him - it was exactly how the demon had recalled. Lucifer found himself standing at the edge of the forbidden past. *His* past.

Lucifer set his mind on his office and attempted to translocate out of there. No luck. He turned back and tried to return to the spot where he woke up. Everything looked the same, the bodies he woke up next to, seemed the same. The not cold, not hard, not earthly Earth looked the same.

He ran further in the other direction, looking for a portal or door of some kind to get back to where he belonged. Nothing. Lucifer kept ending back at the water's edge again. Every direction yielded the same infuriating conclusion.

He was on some kind of bizarre, otherworldly island, surrounded by beautiful naked men. At any other juncture of history, it would've amount to a fantastical dream come true, but knowing what he did, all Lucifer could feel was panic.

"Shit!" he yelled.

He knew he screamed. Lucifer heard himself say it, but there was no indication outside of his own head that a sound had even emerged from his mouth. Nothing for the sound to bounce off of. No sense of airwaves to carry it. He was in some kind of hermetically sealed vacuum. Maybe it was only an illusion, but every fiber of his body responded to the place as if it was real. He pinched himself so hard his skin broke, and blood filled the indentations of where his nails had been. Lucifer saw it with his own eyes. He felt it through his own nerve endings. He swore again, even louder this time, screaming to the inside of his mind.

"Fuuuucccckkkk!"

He nudged the bodies around him with his foot. "Hey, wake up." Softly at first, but soon with more panicked aggression. He bent down low, his balls and cock swinging vulnerably between his thighs as he squatted and shook someone by the shoulders.

"Wake the fuck up… Tell me where I am."

The bodies all moved when he shook them, but none woke. He tried to pull the cloaks away from their faces, but they had adhered with such force that no amount of effort could dislodge them.

He went from body to body, shaking limbs, squeezing balls, pinching nipples… anything to rouse them from their slumber. Not one of the sleeping bodies responded.

It took him a while to go through them all – Lucifer couldn't say how long it had been, but he was exhausted from his efforts. The sun was no higher up in the sky than it was when he woke. Maybe it was always in the same place wherever the place he was in was.

Lucifer sat down in defeat. He had a big problem on his hands and needed to find a solution. There was no way he could think straight with his heart racing as it was, so he took some deep breaths and worked towards bringing himself back to a state of calm.

No sooner had he collected himself than he felt a hand on his back, and the sudden shock and surprise nearly sent him into cardiac arrest.

"Motherfucker sonofabitch," he roared as he spun around in terror.

"Hey Luc," Gabriel said. "Sorry, did I scare you?"

Lucifer's chest was heaving as he was trying to calm himself down from having the living shit scared out of him - not an easy thing to when his pulse began to rise once more at the sight of Gabriel's naked body before him. Something he had dreamed of seeing a million and one times but had never actually witnessed before.

His pulse wasn't the only thing rising.

"I don't get scared," he bluffed, "I get even. Are you only just waking up now?"

Gabriel shrugged. "I like to sleep in a bit

on Sundays."

"Is it Sunday?" Lucifer asked, slipping his cloak on as nonchalantly as he could. Thankfully it was loose-fitting, so his pecker didn't stick out like a railroad crossing gate.

"Of course. Yesterday was Saturday. We met at the club and went to the playground. Don't tell me you've forgotten about all that?"

"I haven't forgotten that," Lucifer assured him, trying to stop himself from staring at Gabriel's beautiful blond pubic hair and stunning genitalia. "But was it yesterday?"

Gabriel's expression shifted. "I think... I think so."

"What do you remember after our little tête-à-tête-à-tête with His Royal Pain in the Ass?"

Gabriel frowned, trying to recall. "It went dark, then light again, and..."

"And..."

Gabriel gestured around, silently admitting to Lucifer that he simply woke up here. *Shit, he doesn't know how we got here either.* Lucifer stood up.

"Where are we?" Gabe asked, his tone

suggesting that the place seemed as strange to him as it did to Lucifer.

"On the edge of our past, as far as I can tell," Lucifer said. "Where Haures and Raziel got to go on the little errands we sent them on."

Gabriel looked as if he was about to protest when Lucifer held up a hand. "I know all about it, Gabe. Great minds think alike."

Gabriel nodded. "And all these magnificent creatures around us?" He asked, sweeping his arm wide to include the hundreds of sleeping, naked men.

"The lost souls, I'm guessing. They're all enjoying the sleep of the dead, as far as I can tell. We could flip them over and fuck them senseless, and they still wouldn't wake up."

Gabriel gave Lucifer a skeptical look.

"And no, I haven't tried it," Lucifer said, then couldn't resist adding with a smile, "at least not yet."

"The day is young," Gabriel said, nodding his head towards the sun, causing his upper body to stretch showing off his form. Lucifer noticed, because how could he not, that Gabriel's clock was starting to twitch as if it was going to stiffen. If it did, Lucifer wasn't sure how much control he might have, or if he'd be inclined to climb Gabriel like a tree and sit on it. *Which is not a good idea until we know where we are.*

"Gabe, would you mind?" He said, indicating Gabriel's cloak. "It's difficult enough to concentrate as it is."

Gabriel looked down, smiled a sexy blush, uttered a half-hearted 'sorry,' and donned his cloak. Even in that unforgiving potato sack, Lucifer found him stunning.

"The day is forever young here," he added in response to Gabe's earlier comment. "That sun - or whatever it is - hasn't moved up or down since I've been up."

"And how long has that been?" Gabriel asked.

"Hours," Lucifer said, then gave it some thought. "Maybe days. I really don't know. This place, whatever, wherever, and whenever it is, is proving to be a total mind fuck."

Gabriel looked ahead to the water.

"That's the boundary Raziel spoke of. Have you tried to cross it?"

Lucifer shook his head. "No, I haven't. I've been too busy sorting out where I am to worry about where to go next. I can't see any way back home."

Gabriel looked around as he walked towards the water's edge. "There isn't a way back home. We've got what we asked for, I reckon. There's no going back now."

Gabriel arrived at the water's edge, and Lucifer quickly caught up to him. They both looked across.

"Pretty fucking wide river if you ask me," Lucifer commented.

Gabriel, beginning with a low, quiet voice, sang a familiar song.

The water is wide, I can't cross o'er,

And neither do I have wings to fly,

Give me a boat, carry two,

And both shall row,

My love and I.

"Didn't know you were a singer, Gabriel," Lucifer said. He was impressed.

"Oh, I'm not really," Gabriel replied, still starring at the expanse of water, "not to speak of, anyway."

"Maybe stick to playing the trumpet, then," Lucifer said, slapping him on the back. Teasing was his go-to way of trying to hide his nervousness and anxiety.

"I have no wings," Gabriel said as he swiveled his hips towards Lucifer, indicating a back free of feathery appendages. "I'll be your boat if you'll be mine?"

Lucifer took a deep breath, swallowed loudly, and exhaled by blowing through his lips, horse-like.

"So, this is the Master, you figure?"

"We did ask Him," Gabriel reminded him. "And He did try to warn us but complied in the end. So yeah, I'd say it's all part of His divine plan to grant our wish."

Lucifer looked down at the water with hesitation.

"After you," Gabriel said.

The demon lowered his barefoot and felt the refreshing cleanse of water against his skin. It was neither cold nor hot, but just right. He laughed.

"What's so funny?" Gabriel asked.

"Nothing. It just all suddenly feels like

we're caught in some pornographic version of *Goldilocks and the Three Thousand Bears.* But I'm sure this will have a much more interesting plot twist, so without further ado, here goes nothing!"

Lucifer jumped into the just-right water, his ears filling quickly with fluid as his head submerged, which meant he wasn't able to hear the splash Gabriel made when he followed suit and jumped in right after him.

Chapter Nine

After enjoying a few moments under the clear waters, Gabriel finally came up for air.

He had planned to take a deep breath, and swim the first length of the river underwater, then switch to a front crawl freestyle stroke to get across the rest of the way. It had been ages since he'd been swimming. Swimming as a viable commuting practice, getting from point A to point B in water, was not all that common throughout human history. After all, that was what boats were for, and, being an angel, Gabriel could fly across bodies of water with no more effort than it took to think. So, traversing a body of water with his arms and legs, having to take the effort to breathe and subsequently hold that breath, was a relatively new concept to him, one that he relished the idea of exploring and enjoying to its fullest potential.

He was looking forward to being able to feel the water as it caressed against his skin, to coordinate his movements and his breath in perfect unison, to feel the strange sensations in his chest associated with needing air and pushing the boundaries until he allowed his lungs the opportunity to gasp a sip... It would appear that he relished needlessly, as it turned out.

No sooner had he come up for air, Gabriel realized he was already on the other side of the river. What had appeared to be a mighty expansive river at first glance turned out to be nothing more than a deep stream. In and out. Gabriel was almost disappointed. The idea of swimming had taken root in his brain and now... he didn't need to.

He kicked out his legs, maybe he could enjoy the water anyway, but as soon as he did his feet landed on stone steps, his body forced into walking up them without him thinking about it. To his left was Lucifer, also walking up the same steps. From the glance he got from Lucifer it seemed his demon counterpart was just as surprised about the lack of swimming, although Lucifer seemed happy about it.

They arrived at a place that was familiar to them both.

"The amphitheater," Gabriel said. "Our old meeting hall. Do you recognize it?"

"Like it was yesterday," Lucifer nodded. "And I'm not just saying that. It genuinely feels like we never left."

"Yes," Gabriel agreed. There was something more than memory in the air though. Like he was both the archangel who had presided over the celestial realm for untold millennia and a member of the original angelic cohort who had never left. "It's like we've been in both places all this time. Never leaving but always gone."

"Eternity is a magnificent mind-fuck," Lucifer said. "You've grown a bit too used to the idea of Time, old man."

Gabriel chuckled. "Speak for yourself," he said and then took in a deep breath of air. "We're back where it all began. I must admit I am not quite sure where to start, but I guess let's go poke around and see what we can discover."

They walked along the water's edge, admiring the architecture of the amphitheater that blended seamlessly into the natural setting, incorporating trees and rocks as part of the construction, so one couldn't tell where nature ended and design began.

Lucifer kept scratching his neck. "This fucking cloak is driving me crazy. Isn't yours itchy as perdition?"

Gabriel shrugged. It was coarse against his skin, but he could easily ignore the discomfort. "Take yours off if you like," he said.

Lucifer stopped walking.

"What?" Gabe asked.

"Wouldn't that be... I don't know... a little awkward?" Lucifer suggested.

Gabriel smiled. "Not for me. Have you forgotten a time before clothes Lucifer? You have nothing to be ashamed of."

Lucifer rolled his eyes.

"I mean... not *nothing*," Gabe stammered. "You have more than nothing. *Substantially* more than nothing. Here, I'll take off mine, so you won't feel alone." Without thinking, he pulled off his cloak and threw it far into the water.

He stood before Lucifer, in his full naked glory, and enjoyed the hungry eyes that took him in. He hadn't been looked at like that since... well... since *ever*! Regardless of what they discovered as they wandered warily down the forbidden memory lane, it was nice to be free of restrictions for once - no protocols, no rules. If there was a chance that Lucifer would never see him again after it was all over, Gabriel wanted to ensure that the love of his life saw him now. All of him.

"Fine," Lucifer said and bent over to pull his cloak off from behind, over his head, and down to his knees.

Gabriel tried not to laugh as the coarse material caught on Lucifer's clearly erect cock as it fell, hanging momentarily on the prodigious fleshy coat hook.

Lucifer blushed and hastily bundled the cloak in his hand and attempted a throw it into the water as well. He misfired, and it landed a few feet away.

"Oh, for fuck's sake," Lucifer said and was about to try again when Gabriel took his hand.

"Let's move on, shall we?"

They entered the great hall and beheld their fellow angels milling around. Everyone was fully nude, so the two visitors blended in. Lucifer was staring at the gorgeous bodies, and Gabriel noticed that the Lord of the Underworld unconsciously kept his hands over his groin.

"I don't think they can see us," Gabriel remarked. "We don't exist to them.

We're revisiting a time and place that we've already left, remember?"

Lucifer tested this theory by going closer to someone. He kept moving his head to try and establish eye contact and snapped his fingers loudly to get attention. The innocent angel ignored him completely.

"Convinced?" Gabe asked.

"Not yet," Lucifer said. He then reached out to touch the angel. His hand pressed into the angel's chest and slowly slid down to his perfect washboard abs and beyond to the promised land - No reaction whatsoever.

"Well, that settles it," Lucifer said. "We've got a free pass to ogle and grope with the old gang. They can't see, hear, or feel us."

"Either that, or he's just not into you," Gabriel joked.

Lucifer rolled his eyes once more. "Aren't you a bundle of wisecracks and jabs, Mr. Mighty Archangel? Let's not forget why we're here, okay."

Gabriel smiled and gave a conciliatory nod. Lucifer was right. Gabe was essentially on probation with him as they sought out the truth of what happened. It just felt so wonderful to be this carefree for the first time - in what felt like a very long time - in Gabriel's long existence. And to be in the place where it all began with the one he has secretly loved all that time; it was easy to forget the seriousness of their journey.

"I haven't forgotten," Gabriel whispered and turned his focus away from Lucifer, letting his eyes scan the room. In addition to seeing the familiar bodies - bodies that were even more perfect than those they left behind, soundly sleeping - hearing the sounds and smelling the air, there was something uniquely familiar about this particular time in this particular place.

"Oh, my heart," Gabe whispered when he recognized why. They were at the gathering for the announcement. Of course! Like a bloodhound, he turned his head sharply to the right and spotted a pair of angels standing together on a rock. "No!" he gasped as he started walking towards them.

"Gabe? Where are you going?" He heard Lucifer's voice but didn't turn around.

A few steps later, there they were.

There *he* was. Gabriel stood in shock, as solid as if he was now carved from stone, as he beheld himself from another time.

"We haven't changed a bit," Lucifer whispered beside him, "and yet, we're completely different."

Gabriel nodded slowly, unable to take his eyes off himself.

"You look unbearably gorgeous here," Lucifer remarked.

"So do you."

"Why is that?" Lucifer pondered.

"Innocence," the archangel said. "There's nothing more attractive. Pure, virginal innocence, unstained by the slings and arrows of the outrageous fortunes of men, angels, and demons. We're not weighed down by responsibility, by the mechanics of existence, or the ways of the world. To see ourselves in this state, to be able to revisit it all... what a gift we've been granted."

Lucifer nodded slowly in agreement, then scoffed. "Don't get too lulled by the beauty of it all," he said. "Remember who's orchestrating it. I don't trust Him as far as I can spit. The other shoe is going to drop, and when it does, all the weight of what we've known and done will press down on us so relentlessly we'll likely be crushed by the burden of it all."

"Or transformed," responded Gabriel, ever the optimist, "like coal to diamond."

"I wouldn't hold your breath," Lucifer snorted. "I may be the Supreme Lord of Lies and Deception, but never forget that I learned from the best."

Gabriel studied the expression on his other self's face, looking deeply into his own eyes.

"He's just made the announcement," Gabriel said, "the Master has just told us of the creation of man." He turned to Lucifer, who was looking at himself with more intent now. "Do you remember you turned to me and said-"

"*Everything will change from this moment onward*," Lucifer quietly intoned and then looked to Gabriel. "Sometimes, I hate being right."

Others in the angelic cohort begin to shuffle off, going back to whatever it was they were engaged in before being called in for the announcement. The innocent versions of Gabriel and Lucifer, however, remained where they were. Soon, they were all alone in the great hall. All alone except for their later selves watching them.

"What was running through your head at this time?" Lucifer asked. "Do you recall?"

"No," Gabriel whispered. "This might be our first revealed memory. Let's watch, listen, and see."

The two visitors took a step back and silently observed their former selves.

"I don't want things to change," Gabriel finally said. "I like things exactly as they are. Why do they have to change?"

"I don't know," Lucifer replied. "I can't explain why they will. I just know it's going to happen."

"You've always been more connected to Him than the rest of us," Gabriel said, without jealousy or judgment.

"Have I?"

"I think so. It seems that way. You love him more, maybe? Or differently?"

Lucifer shrugged. He didn't have an answer.

"Does He think things will change?" Gabriel asked.

Lucifer opened his mouth to respond, but no words came out. He furrowed his brow in thought. "He must. Why else create a new being? Maybe things aren't meant to stay the same forever."

Gabriel shook his head and sat down slowly on the rock. Lucifer placed a hand on his shoulder.

"Is everything okay? You don't look so well."

"I feel something... different. Inside," Gabriel spoke softly. He was tapping his chest with his finger. "What is this? What's happening?"

Lucifer sat beside him. "Maybe this is the change. Starting already."

"I do not like this, not one little bit," Gabriel whispered.

Lucifer wrapped his arms around Gabriel.

"Do you feel it as well?" Gabriel asked, growing more and more frightened. "Can you feel it inside here?" He asked, touching his hand to Lucifer's chest.

Lucifer gasped at the touch. He reacted as if such a gesture had never happened before.

The observing Gabriel looked to Lucifer. "Do you remember any of this?"

Lucifer shook his head in shock. "Not a single bit of it, and trust me, I wouldn't forget being touched like that, especially considering it appears it was for the first fucking time ever!"

"Shh, I'm speaking again."

"What's happening?" Gabriel asked, his hand still pressing against Lucifer's chest, his fingers starting to massage the skin.

Lucifer could barely speak. "I don't know, but it wouldn't be happening if He didn't want it to. I don't think we should be afraid."

"Are you? Afraid?"

"No," Lucifer said after a moment of thought.

"Fucking liar," the observing Lucifer chuckled.

"Would you please shut up?"

"Promise me we'll always stay together. Side by side as we belong."

"I promise," Lucifer said. "I'll never leave you."

"I'll never leave you either," Gabriel echoed, taking Lucifer's hand, which was trembling, and pressing it to the side of Gabriel's face.

Lucifer's hand wandered from the cheek, his fingers snaking through Gabriel's hair.

At that moment, Gabriel leaned in, still with a hand on Lucifer's chest, and pressed his lips to Lucifer's mouth.

"Holy fuck!" Lucifer cried in astonishment.

"Our first kiss," Gabriel was going to count the memory as a blessing even if Lucifer didn't.

"Not just *our* first kiss," Lucifer was bellowing now. "It was *the* first fucking kiss in the history of forever. It was us!"

"No wonder the Master didn't want us to remember this," Gabriel said. "Could you imagine how unbearably torturous our lives would have been knowing we had this moment between us all that time ago?"

Lucifer looked warmly into the archangel's eyes. "It hasn't exactly been a cakewalk, Gabe," he said, "but yeah. I guess we were spared some pain by not knowing the depths of how things were between us."

The two of them turned back to see what was going to happen next, but their vision was suddenly blocked by a wall of water.

Gabriel thought for a moment, he might have been crying over the beauty of the lost memory, but he quickly realized he was back in the river, submerged in the cosmic current surrounding the long ago.

And true to his word from once upon a time, Lucifer was right there beside him, air bubbles rising up from the grin that unraveled across his face.

Chapter Ten

Lucifer hated the water and avoided it at all costs. Showers were quick and efficient for him, and he wouldn't have been caught dead in a bathtub. The phobia may or may not have been influenced by one of Lucifer's beloved Underworld party mates, one he had known when he lived as the Marquis de Sade. The original sadist spoke eloquently and terrifyingly of the murder of Marat in his bathtub, which creeped the shit out of Lucifer, and he had avoided water at all costs ever since.

But now, he was forced to take the plunge into the river of eternity every time the scene changed in the past. It would take him longer and longer to recover after every transitional dip. It didn't make it easier watching Gabriel cavort around like a fucking dolphin in the South Pacific during each swim.

Bloody show-off.

The next scene, after witnessing the first kiss in the pre-history of man, angel, or demon, was even more colossal in its historical significance.

His pre-fall self was alone with the

innocent Gabriel. They had found a secluded spot, away from the rest of the cohort, and were exploring the sensations of pretending to be human. All too human, it turned out.

This time, however, Lucifer found himself more deeply connected to the memory. He could feel what was happening as if he was reliving it versus simply watching it.

"Do you feel this?" he asked Gabriel.

"It's like I'm right there with you over there," Gabriel said, gesturing to their former selves. "I know we're just watching the memory take place, but when your hand - his hand, Lucifer's hand - touches me there, I feel it *here*… Now."

"Same…," Lucifer said. "Maybe we'll kiss again and get to feel that?"

At that moment, the observed Lucifer tentatively put his face on Gabriel's for a second kiss.

The observing Lucifer licked his lips after the kiss was over, savoring the sensation. "Not bad for the first time, but certainly not my best kiss. I've gotten better since then."

Gabriel smiled. "Maybe I'll get lucky and

convince you to prove that assertion."

Lucifer squirmed at the mixed feelings of remembering, feeling, watching two others discover the joys of kissing, and keeping his current love for Gabriel in check as the truth is revealed.

"It's like *A Christmas Carol* meets *Total Recall*," Lucifer said. "What a fucking trip."

"More like *Brainstorm* than *Total Recall*," Gabriel added.

"Never heard of it," Lucifer whispered.

"Natalie Wood's last film. You'd like it. Christopher Walken co-stars."

Lucifer smiled. He used to watch *The Prophecy* over and over again simply because Walken played the archangel Gabriel in the film. It was the most bizarre cinematic turn-on he'd ever experienced.

"I'll be sure to check it out," Lucifer softly spoke. "But let's watch this first. You're much better at playing yourself than any actor. I don't care how devilishly handsome they are."

The two angels stepped shyly into unchartered territory. After their first kiss in the great hall, they knew there was more to be discovered, but neither had any idea of how to start. Where to start.

Lucifer, always the more advanced, the more adventurous of the two, took the lead. Though he was smaller in stature than his partner, he didn't let that deter him from dominating their exploration.

Lucifer ran his hands down Gabriel's chest, exploring with every caress, watching his partner's face intently as it responded to his touch. Gabriel was lost in the all-new sensations that coursed through his body and began to mimic Lucifer's touch so he could enjoy the energy flowing through his body too.

After some time of touching nipples and arms, hips, and thighs. Lucifer, always the braver of the two, gently stroked his hands across Gabriel's pelvis, slowly stroking down until he touched the already very erect cock. He slowly continued his exploration. Watching intently as Gabriel's face melted into the sensations pouring through his body.

"What is all of this?" Gabriel asked after a few moments, "I've never seen any of the others touch like this?"

"I'm not one hundred percent sure what

any of this is," Lucifer replied, hesitating for a moment but not completely removing his hands from where they fell on Gabriel's body. "Do you want me to stop?"

Gabriel hesitated as if considering his options. "No, I don't think I want you to stop, it feels right, my body is exploding with sensations that it has never felt before, and I want to share them with you, I can't imagine having these feelings with anyone else, and I want you to feel what I do too." With those words, Gabriel took a breath and began to caress Lucifer's groin and inner thigh, tickling and teasing until his hand found its way to Lucifer's swollen cock.

The pair pushed and pulled against each other, allowing one hand to graze nipples and necks, pull on ears, and stroke jawlines, while the other remained on the throbbing penis, feeling the sensations surge within their aching bodies.

Lucifer pulled Gabriel down to the ground and moved his kissing lips slowly down Gabriel's body until his mouth reached where his hand had been playing. He wrapped his mouth around Gabriel and slowly licked and sucked. Gabriel cried out, causing Lucifer to stop abruptly. "What happened? Did I hurt you?"

"No, no, no, not at all – my whole body is on fire, it tingles and courses through my body as if lightning is trapped inside, trying to find somewhere to escape. "Let me show you."

Gabriel repositioned himself so he could show Lucifer exactly what he meant. "You taste so good," Gabriel murmured, "there is a strange liquid coming out as I suck, and it has to most incredible flavor. Neither sweet nor savory, but definitely you."

"I found the same when I was sucking you," replied Lucifer in between gasps. He felt his toes curling, and he tracked the energy coursing through his body until it circulated in his groin threatening to explode.

Lucifer let his free hand explore until it found the warmth of Gabriel's heat, he gently probed with his fingers until he found a gap he could nestle inside, and slowly, with patience and care, he stretched the hole until he felt sure he could insert himself inside.

"I want to try something, dear one, will you let me?"

"If it's going to feel like this, you can do whatever you want, bringer of Light."

"Okay then, turn around, so your back is to me."

Gabriel looked confused for a moment but putting the puzzle pieces together, he realized that Lucifer was going to go inside of him. He slowed his breathing in anticipation; Lucifer stroked down his back, stroking his hips and outer thighs as he continued to finger more deeply inside Gabriel.

Lucifer had used some of the sticky liquid dripping from his penis to soften things up as he worked with effort and care, he did not want to hurt Gabriel in any way. Eventually, Lucifer knew it was time, and he gradually and tenderly began to insert himself into Gabriel. He felt the heat envelop him, and the pressure on all sides made his heart and cock swell. He slowly rhythmically began to pulse in and out, letting the sensations build within him. He watched as Gabriel rose and fell with him, making strange and beautiful sounds of ecstasy.

When Lucifer felt he was unable to control himself any longer, he reached around and held Gabriel's cock firmly, pulsing along with the beat of his thrusts, slow and deliberate yet firm and strong. They rode along together until Lucifer felt the sticky liquid run down his hands, and Gabriel groaned in pleasure. Finally, Lucifer released his control and felt his own fluids erupt inside Gabriel, a sense of release and wonder buzzed through his entire being.

The pair collapsed in each other's arms, covered in sweat, saliva, and this strange glossy liquid that they had both discharged from their bodies, a mixture of confusion, elation, and deep connection coursed through them.

"What was that?" Lucifer asked as he gazed into Gabriel's eyes, unable to keep his hands from wandering across the angel's muscled body.

"I have no idea," Gabriel grinned. "But I would happily do again with you by my side, for all eternity."

Sticky and smiling, the pair curled up in each other's arms, neither one fully comprehending the magnitude of what had just happened between them. The angel full of light fell asleep thinking about how blissful it felt to hold his lover in his arms, clinging to each other, to have felt and touched one another, to have been one even for a short time. His lover fell asleep thinking about how strange it was that they had separated themselves from the group, how the sensations had felt in his body, and wanting to understand more about them. Neither fully understood that this moment signified so many firsts for the world and kick-started a chain reaction of many other firsts still to occur.

Lucifer and Gabriel sat with their jaws hanging at their knees. He couldn't speak for the archangel, but Lucifer felt every lick, every touch, tasted every drop of sweet Gabriel sweat on his tongue as he watched himself play with his beloved.

"What do you make of that?" he asked an equally stunned Gabe.

"I… uh… you and I…" Gabriel stammered. "I don't know what to say, Luc. As the designated voice of the Master Himself, I'm at a complete and utter loss for words."

"No shit," Lucifer replied.

"What do you make of it all?"

"I honestly can't be too sure," Lucifer said with a mixture of pain and passion in his voice. Trying to regain his composure, "but I look shorter," the demon finally replied. "I must have grown a bit since all this."

"No," Gabriel quickly responded. "You're the exact same, physically anyway, now as then. As am I."

"Are you sure? I look really short."

"Well…" Gabriel paused, "it's clear where all your height went. Trust me, you're long enough where it counts. I'm amazed I could still walk after all that."

"Maybe that's why you were gifted wings," Lucifer remarked.

Their former selves were sleeping now, wrapped in sticky peacefulness in one another's arms. The look of innocent bliss on each of their faces was never to be forgotten.

"So, does this mean we were mated way back when?" Lucifer finally asked.

"It certainly appears that way. According to the rules set forth by the Master," he said.

"The same Master who wiped this little detail from both of our memories? Clearly, He wanted us to start as separate beings, not joined together as one."

Gabriel nodded. "True. But I don't know the laws around this. I doubt that amnesia serves as a justifiable defense for committing transgressions."

Lucifer's face went red. "Transgressions? What the fuck are you talking about?"

Gabriel patiently shrugged one shoulder. "Oh, I don't know. You've slept with a billion others since this moment, as you know. I've remained devoted."

"Devoted? What the fuck are you saying, Gabriel?" Lucifer was on the verge of blowing up. "Are you telling me you remembered this joining and kept it from me all this time? Not very fucking angelic of you, is it?"

Gabriel could feel himself getting defensive. "Not at all. I don't remember any of this. But, for reasons beyond my understanding or control, I've not fucked a single soul since this moment. Which is more than we can say of you."

"So, your purity, as you call it, is no purer than my tarnished reputation. We both started as innocents after my fucking expulsion, so don't try and slut-shame me now. Clearly, if I had known about this, I wouldn't have slept around."

"And yet you did," Gabriel whispered under his breath. "And I did not."

"What was that?"

"Nothing. You're right. We were both innocent. No harm, no foul, and no mating. You're still free to fuck anything with a pulse if you so choose, I won't stand in your way."

Lucifer stood up in anger. "That's not what I'm asking for, and you know it. Why do you have to be so fucking juvenile and immature when it comes to us? You know I've loved you forever but couldn't have you. I could never have you. Angels were forbidden to me and my kind. So, what if I found comfort and release in others? I didn't love them. So, what if I launched a thousand ships filled with semen in the asses, and faces of those unworthy? I couldn't have the one I wanted, the only one I ever wanted, so I tried to satisfy myself with thousands I *didn't* want. It never fucking worked."

"Luc, I," Gabriel started, but Lucifer continued on.

"And who made that fucking rule, you ask? The Master. The same one who somehow allowed us this delicious historical tryst then took it away from us. It was He who decreed 'thou shalt not' when it came to demons taking angels and angels taking demons. It was always He. Him. It. That son of a bitch's fingerprints are all over every bit of grief and sorrow and loss I've ever known. I'll never forgive Him. Never!"

"Shut up for a second," Gabriel said.

"Don't tell me to shut up," Lucifer felt as though he wanted to yell loud enough so the whole world could hear. "It's time we spoke the truth to that heavenly bastard."

"Look!" Gabriel forced Lucifer's face around to see what he saw.

A figure was approaching the sleeping lovers, calling out to them and rousing them from their post-coital slumber.

"Love to you both," the figure called out.

Lucifer and Gabriel both wake, their eyes opening and instantly taking in the position of their bodies in relation to one another. They untangle arms and legs and stand some distance apart.

"Love to you as well," they say in unison.

"Fuck me," Lucifer says. "It's Malphas!"

The angel they know now as Malphas stops and looks at them both with confusion.

"I am sorry to wake you," he said tentatively, "but we were gathering for the evening feast and noticed you were missing. That you both were missing."

When he said 'both,' Malphas tilted his head in suspicion.

"We fell asleep," Lucifer tried to explain.

"But it's not sleeping time," Malphas countered, "besides, sleeping is something done alone. You were asleep… combined."

"We should go to the feast," Gabriel suggested, "I suddenly feel hunger. Are you not hungry?" he asked Lucifer.

"Very. Let us go altogether."

The two took some steps away, but Malphas stood, his eyes examining the spot where they previously lay.

"Are you not coming along?" Lucifer asked.

"There is a scent in the air," Malphas exclaimed, *"one I am not familiar with. And a kind of dampness where you were lying."*

"We went for a swim," Lucifer tried to explain, *"and must have overexerted ourselves and fallen asleep. But thank you for seeking us out. It would have been a shame to miss the evening feast."*

He started to walk again, but Malphas remained.

"You do not like to swim," he said to Lucifer. *"And besides, swimming is something we all do together. Like eating. Singing. Attending the forums in the great hall. Always together. All of us. The one thing we do alone, separate from everyone else, is sleep. And yet..."*

He looked again to the spot, then slowly back up to the two of them.

"Best to let it go," Lucifer said to Malphas, *"and move on. Come. I'll walk with you to the feasting room."*

Gabriel watched as Lucifer led Malphas off. He smiled nervously when he saw Luc look back in confusion and fear.

"Well, that explains his vendetta against you," Gabriel suggested after the scene dissolved. "Even with his memory wiped out as ours was, something must have lingered in him."

"Tell me about it," Lucifer agreed. "Do you think Malphas knew what we had been doing?"

Gabriel shook his head. "Not a chance. We didn't even know what we were doing while we were doing it. Remember? We're witnessing all the firsts here. First kiss. First fuck. The first bout of suspicion and jealousy. How could he suspect something he knew nothing of?"

"Well, he sure as fuck knew something wasn't right," Lucifer replied. "And he kept that little suspicion alive for all that time, feeding it every chance he got."

Gabriel clapped Lucifer on the shoulder. "We're learning much about ourselves," he said, "and about things we thought were only the domain of man. Desire, jealousy, anger, shame. We're all subject to it, aren't we? Angels, demons, mankind alike."

Lucifer nodded as he held his hand on

the spot where the two of them had been laying, the grass still bent down by their bodies. "I told you everything would change with the creation of man. None of those impulses existed in us until *they* came along."

Gabriel nodded. "Do you still wish they hadn't come along?"

Lucifer thought about it. Before the arrival of man, he'd not tasted sex or fear or power or sorrow. Just a steady, endless parade of bliss.

"No," he finally replied. "Coming back to it all now, I see how fucking boring it all was. We're lucky that His Royal Ass-Wipe did what He did."

"Perhaps," Gabriel conceded. "But it could just be hindsight talking, you know."

"Hindsight is all we have, babe," Lucifer said, slapping his hand on Gabriel's ass as he spoke. "After what I just watched and relived, having a close-up sight of your behind was the best thing that ever happened to me."

"Which you can't remember," Gabriel added.

"Couldn't remember," the demon corrected. "Rest assured, I can remember it now, and I'll never forget it."

"Good to know," Gabriel said as the water level began to rise.

"I mean it, Gabe," Lucifer assured him, looking into his eyes before they were submerged once again. "Whatever we discover next, and whatever it means when we do, I'll never forget what we had back there. Ever."

He couldn't hear what Gabriel said in response, sinking as he was in the water's depth. Lucifer was almost certain, however, that Gabe's mouth was forming the words 'me neither.'

He'd take that.

Chapter Eleven

Gabriel was a bit slower getting out of the water this time. He was enjoying the freedom of being suspended in fluid, floating, neither in the air nor on the ground. He vowed to do more of it when his field trip was over if his field trip was ever over...

"Come on, Gabe," Lucifer called from the shore. "Let's get going."

"In a minute," he replied and dove down for another underwater turn. He could see Lucifer standing on the bank, naked, his arms crossed over his chest in impatience, a foot tapping anxiously on the ground.

Finally, he surfaced and walked slowly out upon the marble steps.

"Take your time," Lucifer snapped, "by all means. Wouldn't want to rush your little dip in the pool."

"Relax," Gabriel said as he tilted his head and pounded the water out of his left ear. "We're in a timeless zone, remember? There is no time to take or lose." He tilted his head the other way and repeated the process - may be a bit too leisurely - with the other ear.

"I don't want to miss anything

important."

"You want to watch us fuck again, don't you?" Gabriel teased. "Pervert."

Before Lucifer could respond, his attention was drawn to the great hall. Gabriel looked up as well. The entire cohort was emerging from the many columned exits, talking amongst themselves. Gabriel listened in on one snippet of one conversation:

"Well, He must *think it's important, or he wouldn't ask it of us," said one angel to another.*

"But allegiance to them? Why would he ask that at all?"

"If that is what He asks, that is what we shall do."

Gabriel grabbed Lucifer by the hand. "We have to find ourselves. Now."

The two of them scanned the crowd but couldn't see themselves anywhere.

"We must still be inside," Gabriel urged. "Let's go."

"So now you're in a hurry all of a sudden," Lucifer moaned as he ran to keep up with his partner, who was bounding into the hall.

The former Gabriel and Lucifer were in the middle of a heated debate:

"I won't do it," Lucifer was arguing. "I swore to bow to none but Him, and I intend to keep my promise."

"But He's changed his mind," Gabriel tried to explain, his voice ever calm and reasonable, "which He has every right to do. These beings He has made; clearly, they mean enough to Him that he would shift his previous commandment. So, who are we to deny His wishes?"

Lucifer looked long and hard into Gabriel's eyes. The young Gabe found it unsettling, for he could see a depth, a struggle in them he'd never detected before. He was surprised to see those eyes become glassy and reddened with water.

"What is this, my love?" Gabriel asked, unable to hide the alarm in his voice. "What is happening with your eyes?"

"I don't know. But they sting suddenly as if rubbed with sand. I am feeling lost."

"Lost? You are here, with me. With all of the others. How can you feel lost?"

Lucifer turned away and walked towards the center of the hall.

"How can you even consider betraying Him?" Gabriel called after. "He who has formed you, who has nurtured you, who has bathed you in love and joy and provided all you could ever need or want? Can you imagine how much pain it would cause Him to have you turn your back after all that He's done for you?"

"But that is exactly my question to you," Lucifer shot back. "Bowing before these creatures, these crude copies of ourselves, would be the worst betrayal of all. Everything that you say, your entire line of reasoning, is what I feel in the opposite direction. How could you consider turning your back to Him and bowing before that which is less than He who made it?"

"But everyone else is in agreement," Gabriel countered. "Why are they able to accept Him at His word, yet you are defiant?"

Lucifer trembled with pain as if he had suddenly been pierced by an arrow in his chest.

"Defiant? Defiant? Is that what you think this is? Defiance is the worst of all transgressions. I could never defy anyone. You. Him. Myself. This is not pride or disobedience, or resistance to something I do not agree with. Please understand. I cannot bow before them. Not I will *not, or I* refuse *to. I simply cannot. My legs will not bend. My head will not lower. I cannot explain why this is the case, but it is. And I thought you would understand. You, of all the others. But I guess I was wrong."*

Lucifer began to run off, and Gabriel pursued him.

The observing couple also followed as fast as they could, not wanting to miss a single word.

"This is it," Gabriel called to Lucifer as he ran, "the moment we've been waiting for. Hurry up!"

Gabriel grabbed his fellow angel's hand, pulling him to a stop.

"You were not wrong," he pleaded, his chest rising and falling in quick succession after the run. "I do understand. It will be a betrayal of Him

if we bow to man."

"I appreciate your support, but you must be sure. I will not force you into a position that you do not believe in."

Gabriel nodded and pressed his hand against Lucifer's cheek.

"I know that. And I thank you. But I now feel as you do. I am with you. I will do as you do."

"How can you be sure?" Lucifer asked.

"How could I feel otherwise? You are my one, my only. We are one and the same."

Lucifer took Gabriel's hand in his.

"So, tell me: why is He asking us to do this? I love Him with all my being, but you… you have always understood Him when many of us struggled with understanding. Why is He asking us to bow?"

Gabriel was stymied by the question. He desperately searched for an answer in his head, his heart, but none was immediately forthcoming. And yet, to not answer would be to raise suspicion in the mind of his partner.

"Why?" Lucifer repeated.

Then suddenly, it came to him. "It is a

test," Gabriel blurted. "To see who is loyal and who is not."

"A test?"

"Think about it. With the creation of a new race of beings, those whom we must assume will be intelligent and possess the means to think and act for themselves... our Lord must be sure who it is that will stand by Him if ever there were to be..."

"... to be... what?" Lucifer implored.

"An uprising? A revolt? I do not know exactly. But my heart is saying this is a test. Bow before man, and we fail. Stand strong before Him, and we shall be exalted by the Master."

"He will treasure us above all others," Lucifer reasoned.

"Yes. We will be his most beloved of all and sit by His side forevermore."

"All because we refused to bow before these creatures," Lucifer said.

Gabriel nodded with enthusiasm. "These creatures will not last," he proclaimed. "He has only created them to serve this purpose of sorting us out. Once he has identified those who He can trust and those who will cave before any whim, *then…" Gabriel flung his hand into the air as if flicking off a fly.*

"Then they are no more," Lucifer nodded in agreement. "Yes, you are right. Once they are gone, we will go back to how things were before."

"Except…"

"Except you and I will be closer to Him. His beloved ones."

"His chosen ones," Gabriel added as the two embraced and held each other tightly.

As the scene dissolved into a watery blur, Gabriel tried hard to reconcile himself to his words and actions from long ago. He couldn't bear to look at Lucifer, knowing that what they both just witnessed must be excruciating for him.

As he watched himself reason and explain, he knew it was genuine. Gabriel couldn't lie. Not now, not then, not ever. He had not fabricated a reason on the spot just to placate Lucifer. But then what happened?

He truly believed what he said. Like it was when he observed their lovemaking earlier, Gabriel was able to feel what his former self felt. He journeyed through the confusion, the desperation to find words to support his answer. He knew that he would not betray Lucifer and leave him to stand alone against the Master.

The suggestion that they were being tested made sense. It resonated deeply within Gabriel, and looking back over the ages, all evidence supported that first assumption. The Master was constantly testing his subjects, demanding love and loyalty above all else. Be they angels, demons, or man. It was entirely consistent with His character to issue that first challenge and expect them to think for themselves. What good were angels who were simply 'Yes Men'?

Gabriel considered his own team of angels and archangels. Autonomy and the ability to think for themselves were paramount in the organizational structure of the realm. It's what Gabriel not only wanted but demanded. And Gabriel was the voice of the Master. Of course, that was what He wanted as well.

And yet.

He looked across in the watery depths of the transition and could see Lucifer's body treading water, his arms and legs gently swaying to and fro, but his head was above the surface.

Gabriel swam towards him, but the closer he thought he was getting, the further away Lucifer appeared. He swam upwards towards the surface.

Once his head was out, he looked all around. There was no sign of Lucifer anywhere.

"Luc?!" He called. "Where are you?"

There was no land, no great hall, no steps to climb out of. Just endless water.

He dove back down and was sure he could see his beloved demon swimming away in the murky distance. He pursued as fast as he could until his angel lungs felt as if they were about to burst. He surfaced again.

"Luc?" He called again.

Nothing. His voice did not echo off anything, lost as it was to the vast, endless water.

He saw the ripples circle out from where he was treading water, but otherwise, the river was as still as glass, the surface pristinely smooth. The sky reflected off it, creating the illusion of an endless mirror of blue and white, white and blue.

Gabriel took a large draw of air into his lungs and dove down once more.

This time he saw others swimming below the surface as well.

Michael, the archangel of Protection, was on his motorcycle, the demon Orobas sitting on the back with his arms wrapped around his mate.

Raphael, the archangel of Healing, holding hands with Seir, the two of them laughing at something one of them had just said.

Uriel and Haures snuggling on a couch, watching a film. Uriel's head resting on Haures' chest. The demon clutching a beer bottle.

Anael and Zagan at the club. Dancing slowly together amidst the flashing lights and pulse of the music only they could hear.

Raziel. Dear Raziel, whom Gabriel had sent here on his behalf. Raziel, whom Gabriel had contemplated destroying once upon a time in order to prevent a mating with Botis. Now here were the both of them, angel and demon joined together. The first mating. The first on the list.

What was all that fuss and fear about? How could anything as beautiful as what Gabriel was now seeing ever have been in question?

The angels and their demon mates faded away as Gabriel swam forward, looking for Lucifer, his intended mate, the ultimate demon, his one and only. He to whom Gabriel promised that he would stand together with.

What went wrong? How could I have gone back on my word like that?

Gabriel's head was heavy with these thoughts. It was an effort to lift it out of the water.

As he did so, his feet found the marble steps below, and the entire shore with its great hall and natural beauty materialized before his eyes.

Chapter Twelve

All the angels were gathered on the shore, just at the top of the marble steps. Lucifer stood at the back and was the only one who could see Gabriel emerge from the water and walk amongst them.

The younger Lucifer and Gabriel were gathered as well, standing apart from each other for the first time. Everyone else was gathered on the shore and not in the great hall. Lucifer picked up snippets of conversation. The Master had called them all here.

The Lord of the Underworld was hurting, and he projected that pain and anger outwards. He couldn't help it. Gabriel, who had known him for millennia, was smart enough - and respectable enough - to keep his distance. He stood on the other side of the crowd.

He wished for many things over his time, Lucifer did, but what he wanted more than anything was to stop this visitation of their past right now. To take Gabriel by the hand, hot on the heels of the promise he made to stand beside Lucifer and never bow to man and escape the inevitable truth that would result in the opposite of that. A truth he was about to witness for the second time.

It wasn't so much the fact of Gabriel reneging on his promise that bothered Lucifer. He could not recall *how* it happened but was pretty fucking solid on the fact that it did. No, what he dreaded was feeling all the qualities around it once more. The knife in the back. The slap in the face. The pain, the humiliation, the trauma of having his one true love reject him. Again.

Fuck it. He'd come this far. Best to see it through.

He looked out over the cohort of angels. All those perfect bodies, tight asses, and innocent faces.

They have no idea what's to come, he thought. *No fucking idea the titanic shift that awaits them. All the greed, power struggles, war, killing, raping, pillaging, and profiting. It's all down-fucking-hill from here.*

He stole a glance over to Gabriel, who he saw was also looking out at the group before them.

And what are you thinking, my beautiful, sad, duplicitous love? How they are about to be ushered into a world of beauty and creativity? All the love, kindness, art, music, tales of valor, heroics, salvation, and sacrifice? Are you thinking that, Gabriel? That they have no idea of the beauty that awaits?

We'll always be on opposite sides of everything, won't we? Black and white. Yin and yang. Chalk and cheese. Forever trying to strike the balance somewhere in the middle.

Lucifer's ruminations continued to build.

Me, the dark King of the Underworld. Lord of Lies. Master Manipulator. Dealer of Deceit. Yet, standing over there, I'm simply the most beloved of the Master and bringer of light. My love will be my downfall. While you, Gabriel, he looked across again, *you are now the Voice of the Master, the Anointed leader of the angels. Lord of the Realm of Light. Yet, standing over there, you're a love-struck coward, about to commit the first act of betrayal in the history of all beings.*

Lucifer shook his head. The contradictions were too much for him to carry on his own.

As he attempted to clear his thoughts of things complex, the voice of the Master began to speak.

"My beloved angels," the voice began, thundering across the heavens, "I have called you here to share with you what is nearest and dearest to my heart. We stand, all of us, on the shore of what is to come. A future that will excite you, challenge you, and transport you to places you couldn't possibly imagine. You all have so much more to give, to learn, to offer, and I have been amiss for too long in denying you the chance to fulfill your potential."

What a load of shit, Lucifer thought to himself. He couldn't give a fuck if the Master heard his thoughts.

"Behold…"

The mist that was hovering above the water suddenly cleared, and a world began to come into focus on the other side. The angels all stood facing out, their focus across the river, and they exclaimed and gasped in wonder and awe at what their eyes beheld.

"Man."

A cohort of bodies stood across the water. They were, in all outward appearances, the same as the cohort of angels witnessing their reveal. Not exact copies, but similar enough. Each man was strong and beautiful. Some were taller, some less so. Some had long flowing hair, others with shorn locks, and still others with no hair at all. Faces with the same features; various shapes of noses; mouths with full lips and white teeth; broad chests and shoulders, muscular arms and legs, and eyes that looked as curiously at the angels as the angels' eyes looked at them.

"These are my beloved children," the Master continued. "They deserve all the love, respect, and reverence you show to me. Please extend it to them."

Lucifer watched as, one by one, the angels bent down, took a knee, and lowered their heads to the standing bodies across the water. He wanted to rush in and yank each and every one back up by their shoulders, forcing them to stay upright, and scream in their faces:

DON'T BE SO FUCKING COMPLIANT!

Instead, he just shook his head slowly in helpless, useless disgust.

Soon all the angels were kneeling. All but two.

Lucifer, of course, who stood tall and confident, defiant, his eyes fixed not on the gathering of man across the water but up to the skies, to the source of the voice. He was at one end of the cohort, on the side where the invisible, observing Gabriel was watching.

And Gabriel, who stood less tall, less confident, his eyes darting nervously to Lucifer, to the skies, to the crowd across the lake. He shifted his weight from foot to foot, clearly in a state of anxiety. He was only a few paces away from the invisible, observing Lucifer. And Lucifer was watching his every move, trying to anticipate and interpret each muscle twitch and eye blink.

"What is this?" the voice cried in anguish. *"Two of my own? Tell me, how have I wronged you that you would hurt me like this?"*

"We seek not to hurt you, my Lord," Gabriel called. *"Only to show you that our love for you is so immense, so pure,*

that it cannot be negotiated away."

Lucifer, however, did not respond. He stood still as a statue, his eyes wide to the sky, filling with tears that streamed down his cheeks.

"But I ask you to show that love to my children now," the Voice said. "Surely, they are as deserving of it as I?"

"We bow only to you, my Lord," Gabriel cried. "To none other than you." He kept his eyes cast down, unable to look towards his master.

"Look at them!" The voice bellowed, "and tell me you don't see me in their eyes and in their hearts. LOOK! I beseech you."

Gabriel lifted his gaze and looked across the water, and smiled like a father beholding his child for the first time.

"Do you see? I am there in their faces. I have made them in my own image. I know you have all asked, at one time or another, for me to share my face as well as my voice. Well, this is my concession to that request. If ever you wish to look upon me, then look upon them, for I am there."

"Oh, my Lord," Gabriel said, his eyes now filling with tears as well. He could

not pull them away from the sight across the water even if he tried.

"Do you see me now?" the voice asked gently.

"I see you, my Lord," Gabriel cried. "I do."

"Then show the love you claim to have for me."

Gabriel's knees buckled and bent as he lowered to the ground as if being pulled there by a force beyond his control.

"NOOOOO!!!" His invisible counterpart cried out. "NO, you promised to stand with him. You promised!"

Lucifer watched as his old friend and confidant, Gabriel the Archangel, ran across the scattering of kneeling bodies and wrapped his massive arms around his former self.

"Do not kneel down," Gabriel cried in desperation, "please don't betray yourself like this!"

Lucifer could see the prodigious strength exerted in Gabriel's arms and back, trying to hold his former self upright. Gabriel, the younger, however, was oblivious to the intervention. He continued to gaze, love-struck, there was no other word for it, at the bodies and faces across the water.

His knees touched the ground, and he extended his arms forward and paid full obeisance to them, burying his face in the earth as he did so.

Gabriel tried and tried to pull him up. Lucifer knew his strength was sufficient to pull mountains apart and lift entire cities off the ground. But he was helpless to move one body fixed in the past.

The archangel looked across to Lucifer. "I'm sorry, my love. I tried. Oh, how I tried."

But Lucifer was no longer looking at him. He was now transfixed by his former self, who still stood tall and proud and filled with light, his eyes imploring the Master to see what true love and devotion actually looked like.

"It is finished," the voice said. "You are too proud, too defiant to show your love to me? Very well. You are no longer worthy of being among the rest. You are no longer worthy of being in my sight. You are no longer worthy of looking

upon my beloved children. My heart breaks for you."

Flames appeared on Lucifer's feet and began to climb up his legs. They spread to his knees, then waist, then chest. In an instant, his entire face and those eyes - those incredible eyes filled with glorious light - ignited.

"Be gone! Out of my sight!"

Gabriel left his prostrate self and ran across to the burning body on the other side of the shore. He tried to wrap his arms around the flames and carry them into the water, but there was nothing there to extinguish. Lucifer was gone. All that remained was a blackened patch of earth and the unmistakable scent of sulfur.

Meanwhile, the contemporary Lucifer stood alone, shaking and convulsing as if in shock. It wasn't as if he had forgotten this moment - quite the opposite. How could he have forgotten? The unbearable pain of rejection, coupled with the burning of angelic flesh and celestial bone, was not an experience one could easily relegate to the halls of experiences forgotten.

And just as he feared, he felt it all again in the here and now. The soothing balm, of course, was watching just how steadfast and strong he was in the midst of it all. That perspective was denied him the first time around. He had nothing to be ashamed of and felt only renewed pride in his unshakeable integrity.

Could it be that Gabriel wasn't weak? Lucifer wondered. Maybe he didn't betray him? Maybe, the truth was that he was coerced. Tricked. Manipulated into bowing against his will. Was it possible that Gabriel simply fell under the spell of the Master, which was next to impossible to resist?

As Lucifer watched his one true love attempt to stop what was happening, what had happened, both with the bowing angel and the burning demon, he felt a surge of pity instead of anger; love instead of hatred; forgiveness instead of scorn.

Gabriel was walking toward him now, crying out that he had tried. That he hadn't wanted to kneel. That he loved Lucifer more than himself, more than the Master, more than anything or anyone or anytime or anyplace.

Lucifer didn't know what to do. Open his arms? Turn away? Spit in his face?

Water filled the scene as the memory dissolved in the waves, and soon those arms he thought might be extended in love were put to work pushing the sea to and fro. He was treading water, something he really truly hated, and not hugging his angel, the one thing he truly desired, and in that moment, as he had many times before since the ordeal with Gabriel began, Lucifer felt his heart sink.

Would this ordeal never fucking end?

Chapter Thirteen

Gabriel climbed out of the river and found himself back on the other side, close to the spot where the adventure had started.

The bodies of men, those first prototypes of creation, were still there, divine in their perfection, looking out across the water at the cohort of angels bowing before them.

The Master must have reduced their likeness to the angels considerably in the next iteration of his creation. Mankind, as Gabriel understood them, was beautiful and majestic, yes, but nothing like the ones he was seeing. The first batch had been abandoned by the Great Creator as He adjusted the recipe like a litter of puppies left to perish in the elements.

But clearly, they did not perish. They continued to mill around, looking across the water, reliving that glorious moment when the angels all bowed to them. All but one.

That one was nowhere to be seen now. Neither version of him. Gabriel couldn't see Lucifer, his colleague, nor the memory of Lucifer, the banished angel amongst the throng of bodies.

A spare cloak lay on the ground. Gabriel picked it up and dropped it over his naked body. He no longer felt free, so what was the point in appearing that way? He was in the space between the past and present; the heavenly and earthly; memory and experience.

Concentrate, he said to himself. *Focus your thoughts.*

Images of Lucifer, alone, pale, shivering in the cold came to mind. He locked his energy on those snippets of recollection and did all he could to move toward them.

The bodies began to disappear, those lost souls stuck forever in a repeated loop of adoration. *Could be worse*, Gabe thought. *If one has to endure an eternal Ground Hog Day, that's about as good as it gets.* Adoration. Reverence. Love.

The scene was changing rapidly. All signs of greenery and waterfront life washed away, replaced by barren wilderness. It felt like he was on the surface of the moon. Gabriel felt the temperature change as the air-cooled, the warmth of the sun dissipated to nothing. He could sense it but was not affected by it physiologically. But emotionally and psychologically, he could feel the impact.

A wasteland. Of course. He remembered being here, seeking out his companion once upon a time. And just like that, the memory came to life. There he was with Lucifer, holding his love's hand, trying to explain the inexplicable.

"The fallen?" Lucifer repeated. "He said that?"

"Yes. He said, 'who better to tend to the fallen but he who has fallen himself?' That is the role He has entrusted to you."

"How kind of Him," Lucifer nodded. "The damned leading the damned."

"You're to have your own kingdom. None of the others were assigned a kingdom."

Lucifer looked into Gabriel's eyes. "And you? What is your fate?"

"I am to be the Voice and Hero of the Master. All communication between Man and the Master will go through me."

Lucifer nodded. "Well," he said. "You're the highest of the high. And I'll be the lowest of the -"

"No, don't say that," Gabriel shook his head. "Any one of us could have taken my job. Only you could be entrusted with the souls mired in darkness. You will bring them light, Lucifer."

"Lucifer?" He repeated.

"That is your name now," Gabriel explained. "The Bearer of Light."

"And yours?"

"Gabriel."

"Of course. Man of the Master," Lucifer said. "It seems you made the right choice, Gabriel. Bowing before them."

"Please don't be angry with me," Gabriel beseeched him. "I never meant to betray you. Please believe me."

Lucifer was silent for a long time. "I thought we were agreed," he finally said. "I believed you when you said you would stand with me. What changed your mind?"

Gabriel shook his head and lifted his shoulders. "I don't know for certain. It felt like my legs were bending against my will."

"He forced you?"

"No…" the angel replied and then asserted his voice: "it was my choice. I

take full responsibility for it."

"Why are you speaking in this way?" Lucifer asked, searching the angel's eyes for an answer. "This doesn't sound like the one I knew before."

"It is me," Gabriel replied with little conviction, "this is me. One and the same. Always and forever."

"And yet, so different," Lucifer said.

"Best to let it all go, Lucifer," Gabriel said with a stiff nod as if issuing a command, "and move on."

Lucifer smiled in recognition of something.

"What?" Gabriel asked.

"Nothing," Lucifer quietly said, "you're right. Best to move on."

He turned and walked away, unable to shake the ghost of a memory or premonition of a memory to come.

Gabriel followed and turned him around. Lucifer struggled to find something, anything, to say. "At least we'll have each other," he mumbled.

Gabriel stiffened and let go of Lucifer slowly, reluctantly. "About that..." he began to say, but his voice choked, stopping him from getting the words *out.*

"About... what?" Lucifer urged.

"We are forbidden from being together," Gabriel croaked. "For now, forever."

Lucifer laughed out loud. It seemed such a ludicrous thing to consider. "What?"

"It is a new law," was all Gabriel could manage.

"Us being kept apart is a law?" Lucifer barked. "Sounds more like a punishment."

"Not just us," Gabriel continued. "All angels must keep away from you and your subjects."

"Me? But I am an angel," Lucifer cried. "Just like you."

Gabriel shook his head and sobbed.

"Aren't I?" Lucifer shouted.

Gabriel turned his back to Lucifer and lifted his head to the skies above.

"Gabriel? What are you doing?"

White wings appeared on Gabriel's back, fused to his shoulder blades, and spread wide.

"Gabriel?"

The angel spread his wings, wide as the sky, and shot upward, leaving Lucifer alone in this cold, dark world.

"What an exit!"

Gabriel turned around from the frozen memory to see Lucifer standing behind him, his hands clapping together in mock applause.

"Holy fuck did you ever drink deep from the Kool-Aid cup," the demon laughed. "I'm surprised you didn't fucking drown yourself in it."

Gabriel couldn't help but nod in agreement. "I've learned a thing or two since then," he said. "But yeah. I'm most certainly not proud of how that went."

"It sucks being alone, it sucks even more feeling alone," Lucifer commented. "I didn't think I would ever see you again after that. As it turned out, I wasn't able to get rid of you in my life."

"Not so easily, anyway," Gabriel quietly said. "To be honest-"

"When are you not?" Lucifer quickly interrupted.

"Always the jokester, but you are right on that account... As I was saying, I argued with the Master to allow me to work *with* you, not against you. I made sure that we could still see each other and work together going forward. It was the least I could do to ease the suffering of being apart from you. So, I guess at least we had that."

Lucifer was scratching his neck and shoulders madly. "These fucking cloaks," he complained.

"I tried to get Him to lift the ban that stopped angels and demons mating," Gabriel confided, "for centuries, I tried. He wouldn't budge on it. I eventually gave up asking."

"Who can blame you? It must suck to the be the Voice of the Master only to have your voice ignored by the Master it represents, over and over and over and over and over...."

"But I never stopped loving you, Lucifer. I never stopped wanting you. Desiring you. I've not felt that about a single other soul. Not once, in all this time. It's always and only been you."

Lucifer simply nodded, his eyes twinkling with appreciation.

"I want you to know that," Gabriel whispered as the cloak fell from his body onto the ground below. He took a few steps away and turned his back as he did before. Wings appeared behind him, exactly as they did before, and just as he was about to take flight, Lucifer's voice halted him.

"Where the fuck do you think you're going?"

Gabriel, his eyes now filled with tears, turned his head around.

"I don't know," he said. "I haven't thought that far ahead. Someplace where I can be free of the pain of not being with you."

"Does such a place exist, Gabe?" Lucifer asked. "If it does, then, by all means, go there. Let me know if there's any available real estate when you arrive because sure as shit, I'll need to find the same for myself."

Gabriel shrugged, his wings vibrating in anticipation of taking off.

"Why not stay?" Lucifer asked.

"I made a promise," Gabriel replied, "that if it turned out that I had betrayed you in the past, as you suspected, then I would let go and leave you alone for good. I can ill afford to break two promises to you in the course of one existence."

Lucifer held out his hand. At first, Gabriel thought it was extended to him, and his heart did a few backflips, not to mention his cock twitching twice or thrice involuntarily. But it was all for naught when a scroll appeared in that extended hand. It wasn't extended for Gabriel at all. For the hundredth time in recent days, Gabriel was crushed once again.

"Look familiar?" Lucifer asked him.

"The list," Gabriel said. "With the names of six couples green-lighted for mating. Angels and demons."

"It ain't forbidden no more," Lucifer said. "See how that old bugger changes His mind more often than we change our shorts?"

Lucifer proceeded to rip the list to shreds. "But it doesn't matter. I don't need a piece of fucking paper from Head Office to tell me what I already know. What I've known since before forever."

Gabriel tried to pull his wings back in, but they wouldn't budge. He could feel

183

his feet beginning to lift off of the ground, and he had to work like mad to keep his feet planted where they were.

"But if you truly want to go, I can't make you stay," Lucifer added, seeing Gabriel struggle.

"I don't want to go," Gabriel called, "are you kidding? I want to stay and throw myself into your arms, but I can't seem to pull myself out of this state of takeoff."

Lucifer walked towards him. "Poor Gabe. Your body seems to obey some other command when it matters most that you control it. Are you telling me that you physically can't stay here?"

"I'm telling you that I'm trying my best to keep myself here, but there's an unseen force pulling me like a vacuum up there."

"So, you're saying that something's sucking you off the earth, you mean. Shall I get down on my knees and attempt to counter?" Lucifer laughed.

"I'm serious, Luc," Gabriel stammered. "This isn't funny."

"You need to deal with your daddy issues, my friend," Lucifer soberly advised, "or you'll never be able to act on your own free volition."

Gabriel knew he was right, looked up, took a deep breath, and summoned the power of his voice.

"Hear me, Master," he bellowed. "Enough is enough! Let me go!"

"And move on," Lucifer added, calling to the heavens as loudly.

"Please, Luc, let me handle this," Gabriel implored.

Lucifer threw his hands up and stepped away, walked a few paces across from Gabriel, and sat down on the ground facing him.

"I have done everything you have asked of me, right from the beginning. I have been your loyal and faithful servant. Your voice, agent, and intermediary. I have never asked for anything in return, as it has been honor enough just to serve you, but now, I ask you to release me. Please. Allow me the chance to live and love without your hand constantly pulling me back or bending my knee."

Gabriel willed himself to stay on the ground, to stay with Lucifer. He waited for the Master to reply and concentrated on keeping himself low, thinking heavy thoughts.

"Please, if you love me a quarter of what you claim to," Gabriel continued, "If you have any compassion for me at all, you will release me. Has what is destined not been prolonged for long enough? Have Lucifer and I not been your loyal and faithful servants?"

He continued to will himself to stay close to the ground as his wings strained to lift him higher above it.

"Do you not recall your own words to us? 'I want to see demons and angels loving each other in mated pairs for all eternity. Maybe then balance will be restored in this beloved world of mine.'"

He could feel muscle tissue starting to rip as if he were tearing himself in half. The pain was excruciating, but Gabriel refused to back down or give in to the pain, not this time.

"'Don't fail me in this,' you commanded. So? Here I am, once again, moving the stars on the sky and earth itself to not fail you. Must you forever resist that which you bloody well ask for *every fucking time*?"

Gabriel's wings suddenly went limp, and he landed on his ass with a heavy thud. He was covered in sweat from the effort, and his tailbone now ached, but he had done it, he had stood up to the Master and claimed what was rightfully his.

The wind picked up, and Gabriel could hear a voice hidden in it as it swirled around both he and Lucifer, whose hair was swept around his face from the stormy breeze.

The voice, if it was a voice and not merely imagined by Gabriel, whispered three words before a seesaw appeared between Gabriel and Lucifer, the barren nothingness of the wasteland populated now by the familiar surrounds of a children's playground:

As. You. Wish.

Chapter Fourteen

Lucifer took in his surroundings.

Sitting across from him, balanced on the other end of the seesaw, was Gabriel. Not a stitch of clothing on his back.

Lucifer glanced down and could see his own balls and semi-erect cock squished between his legs as his ass cheeks pinched down on the wooden seat of the teeter-totter.

For fucks sake, Master! He thought and then laughed. *At least the old bastard still has a sense of humor.*

Two young children were staring at them, eyes as wide as stars, their mom too engrossed in Facebook on her phone to look up.

"Hey, Gabe," he whispered loudly, snapping the archangel out of his long-ass trip down memory lane. "If you don't mind doing that voodoo you do so well, we could both use a bit of help covering up someone's idea of a joke."

Gabriel shook the cobwebs from his head and looked down with horror.

"Honestly, am I surrounded by giant children," he mumbled as he waved his hand in a quick gesture of reparation.

In an instant, Gabe was covered head to toe in a fine linen suit, and Lucifer felt the familiar denim and red t-shirt hugging his flesh, motorcycle boots on his feet and an elastic suddenly tugging his long dark hair into a ponytail. Gabriel was a man who appreciated attention to detail, after all.

Lucifer looked down and winked at the kids. They ran to their mother, and he could hear them trying to convince her of what they had just seen. She merely nodded, said 'mmm-hmm,' and still didn't bother to look up from her phone.

"So?" Gabriel asked as he lowered his end of the seesaw.

"So what?" Lucifer replied, rising up in the air.

"Here we are, back where we started," Gabe said as he slowly sank to the ground.

And on it went, back and forth, up and down.

"Pretty much," Lucifer nodded. "Only knowing now what we didn't know then."

"Which is what, in your opinion?"

Gabriel asked.

"You betrayed me," Lucifer calmly said, "as I suspected you did."

"Which, as we both saw, was out of my control," Gabriel argued.

"So, you were forced to kneel?"

"I'm not saying it was forced, I'm only saying it's cloudy," Gabriel replied, "and I didn't remember it happening. Nor did you."

"Not remembering is no defense," Lucifer insisted.

"Fair enough."

They paused their exchange for a moment and played up and down like two overgrown children discovering a toy for the first time. Although Lucifer did get lost for a few moments considering some other games, he would rather be playing with his good friend sitting across from him.

"Want to know what *I* have learned?" Gabriel offered.

"Hit me."

"We mated back then. When we were equals. We became one. And you have betrayed me how many times since then? With how many different beings?"

Lucifer stopped the up and down motion and dug his heels into the ground. "That's not the same thing at all," he said, just remembering in time to keep his voice low enough so the children couldn't hear.

"Why not?"

"Because the memory of that…"

"Yes…?"

"It was wiped away from…"

"Mm-hmm? Yes?"

Lucifer knew he had no argument. If amnesia was no defense for Gabriel, it couldn't be one for him.

"So, it's a draw, is it?"

"I'd say so. Even Steven."

"We balance out," Lucifer nodded. "I can live with that."

"So?" Gabriel repeated as he raised himself up.

"So what?" Lucifer replied, lowering down.

"Are we good?"

Lucifer, once down on the ground, swung his leg around and dismounted. He grabbed the seat, however, at the last minute, preventing Gabriel from hitting the hard ground but still making him flinch. The archangel gingerly stepped off.

"I've been thinking, Gabe," he said as the two walked out of the playground. "We love each other. We've already mated. Whether that union holds up in His Holy playbook is beside the point; it holds up in mine."

"Mine too," Gabriel nodded.

"You fucked up," Lucifer continued, "but then so did I."

"We balance each other out," Gabriel nodded, impatient, "right. We've established that."

"Right. Which begs the question: why all the drama? Why the intense trip down memory lane, reliving old events, rehashing ancient traumas? Why would His Nibs bother with it at all?"

Gabriel was nodding along. "You mean what did He have to gain from it all?"

"Yeah," Lucifer said. "Gain or lose, perhaps?"

The Prince of Pain stopped walking and looked out over the water. They were on the shore of the Pacific now, at a place he knew as Alki Beach, the hard rocky sand crunching beneath their feet.

"If we were kept in the dark, and had no inkling of this possible betrayal, don't you think we would have kept going, full steam ahead, into our own mating?"

Gabe nodded in agreement.

"Like I said," Lucifer continued, "He always knew who had my heart, just as I'm sure He knew who had yours. Our names weren't on the original list because He knew we were pretty much sealed to each other anyway. He may be manipulative and a spoiled little shit sometimes, but the Master is not blind. He sees everything. He knew we mated. He knew you promised to stand with me. He knew you would cave - whether he pushed you down on your knees or not. He knew we'd 'remember' all of it and arrive here, where we started, wondering why the fuck He even bothered."

Gabriel nodded with every item on Lucifer's checklist. "Agreed. So why did he bother?"

Lucifer picked up a flat rock and skipped it far across the calm ocean, it continued to bounce along the surface of the water well after it was out of sight.

"I think he kept it from us because he was afraid of being shown up," the demon said.

"By whom?"

"Yours truly, of course," Lucifer replied with a smile as he dusted the dirt from his hands. "His weakness in all of this is a sin of omission. I think it chews away at Him like a mouse nibbling on the anus."

Gabriel rolled his eyes at the grotesque imagery, then raised his brows to ask, 'well?'

"He never forgave me," Lucifer said. "In all this time, you think the Master would have developed enough empathy and sympathy to pull me aside and say, 'hey, brother. I know you thought you were doing the right thing back then, and I've been shitting on you for a gazillion years because of it. I fucked up. I'm sorry. You're ok'. But He never has. Not once."

"Do you expect Him to?" Gabriel asked.

Lucifer shook his head. "No. I mean, yeah, for a long, long time, I sure as fuck did. He could have pulled on his Big Boy pants and apologized. But I

194

don't feel that way anymore. Not after having all the pieces put back in the puzzle of the past."

Lucifer's smile kept spreading. Devilish. Devious. Delightful.

"What?" Gabriel asked, trying to read between the lines to no avail.

"Now that I know you betrayed me, the same way I betrayed him… well, once I forgive you, guess what?"

"Holy fuck!" Gabriel gasped. "You'll be that much better than… holy double fuck."

The sky suddenly darkened, and a terrible hurricane began to blow in off the water.

"Quick!" Gabriel yelled, his voice drowning in the noise of the storm. "Before you can't."

Lucifer remained calm, his hair and body were unmoved by the forces of nature. "It's already done, my friend. And He knows it, too. It's going to drive Him crazy for the rest of forever. Which I'm perfectly comfortable with. I just haven't told *you* yet."

"Are you sure you want to invoke His wrath?" Gabriel cried.

"I'm not afraid of him," Lucifer said with a shrug, "only afraid of becoming like Him, which is what banishing you from my sight would result in. Fuck that, I say."

He looked up into the dark storm and screamed with a joy unhinged. "FUCK THAT!!!!"

Lucifer lowered himself down on one knee, took Gabriel's hand, and looked up at him with those deep, irresistible eyes of his.

"Gabriel, Archangel of all Divine Communication, I forgive your transgressions against me. I harbor no resentment and promise to never bring it up again out of spite or malice. I'm sorry it has taken so long and that we have wasted so many years that could have been better spent. I love you."

The wind stopped, the sky lightened, and the ocean settled.

Gabriel stood as still as marble, hardly able to breathe.

"Done like dinner," Lucifer said with a nod. "Come on, I'll buy you a beer."

As the demon walked confidently along the beach back in the direction of Club AZ, he felt two strong arms wrap themselves around his waist.

"The beer can wait," Gabriel said as he spread his mighty wings and flew up and away, the Lord of the Underworld held tight against his chest.

Lucifer could feel the archangel's hard-on pressing into his thighs as they flew and reached around with his free hand for something to hold on to during the flight.

Chapter Fifteen

The flight to Gabriel's celestial office was fast and efficient, as the blood that was supplying oxygen to his wings was in stiff competition, with blood redirected to sustain his erection.

Upon arrival, he bellowed a command to his entire staff that they had the rest of the week off, only to find it was still the weekend and no one was there.

He kicked open the double doors to his office and threw Lucifer down on the couch. With a snap of his fingers, the Lord of Underworld was naked once again and as hard as granite himself.

"Don't you want to undress me with your own two hands?" Lucifer asked, startled to be so vulnerable so quickly.

"Plenty of time for that, my dear," Gabriel moaned. "Later."

Gabriel pounced onto the couch, landing lightly but forcefully. Lucifer laughed, "Gabriel, my love, you look a little like a demon-possessed."

"I want what's mine, and I want you now!" Gabriel lunged and forced a long passionate kiss, his hands clawing over Lucifer's chest like an animal.

Lucifer, not to be outdone, flipped Gabriel onto his back, switching their places in a blink of an eye. He ripped Gabriel's linen suit from his body, revealing rippling muscles aching to be touched and licked. Lucifer kissed back, firm in his idea to claim his mate, and damn well remember it.

Gabriel licked and kissed, teasing and stroking Lucifer's body, then with a wicked smile and a flick of his fingers, Lucifer found himself with his back on the couch once again.

"If memory serves me, Prince of Darkness, it is my turn to claim you." He winked and moved down Lucifer's body, swiftly sucking the already very erect cock into his mouth and promptly lubing up his fingers with the corresponding pre cum. He dived deep into Lucifer's tight heat with no hesitation. A millennium of waiting was long enough.

Gabriel pulled Lucifer's knees up and slid underneath to get a better position, he dived deep with slick fingers with one hand and owned Lucifer's body with the other, tickling, tempting, stroking, and caressing, it was all too much for Lucifer who just relaxed back onto the couch and let the waves of passion and clear ownership that Gabriel was exuding wash over and through him.

He had to admit he was always the dominant one in all his previous sexual forays, and it was an incredible feeling to have someone strongarm him and release wave after delicious wave of pleasure through his body.

Lucifer looked up and saw Gabriel's adoration glowing in his eyes as he took in with wonder the sight of Lucifer's sweating body writhing beneath him. Lucifer had never in his memories even been looked at like that, he had never had anyone own him, claim him, love and adore him quite like his mate did. He stared straight back into Gabriel's eyes. "You are so fucking picture-perfect in this moment, Gabe; I have been dreaming of this for eternity."

"As have I, my sweet demon, you are my one and only, always have been, always will be, I will never… let you down… ever… again."

Lucifer felt things stirring in him that he thought had died a slow death eons ago. He felt like he was waking up and feeling alive for the first time, he felt loved, owned, and cherished. He planned on returning those feelings to his greatest gift and best friend for long as he had air in his lungs. Air that was quickly escaping him as Gabriel plunged his huge cock straight into his tight slick ass. Both men groaned while Lucifer was quietly amazed he could take all of Gabe's full and impressive girth. It certainly took Lucifer's breath away.

The world stood completely still for a full three seconds as they froze suspended in one glorious moment, both of them recalling their first time, which they could now vividly remember thanks to their recent trip to the long-lost past. As time stopped, just for that moment, they were both their old selves and a being that was very new; in unison, they were joined, they were two parts of one whole being - Yin and Yang, chalk and cheese, in perfect balance.

Gabriel felt a course of electricity course through his body from the top of his head that ran through him directly into Lucifer. As it did, his body took over. Gabriel wanted Lucifer to feel every inch of him, and he needed to make damn sure that neither of them would forget their second claiming... Ever.

He ravaged Lucifer's body, his body surging forward, again and again, and again. Lucifer groaned, his toes curling so sharply that the sheet threatened to shred. Gabriel knew their moment was coming to a close, and he wanted Lucifer to feel every sensation of pleasure he could offer. So, he took a deep breath, slowed his rolling hips down, and reached for Lucifer's cock, pulling it close, so it was wedged between their heaving bodies. Lucifer's back arched, and they both finished together, falling into a heap as they had at the beginning of time. This time not on the grass but on a now very sticky couch.

After the heavy breathing had subsided, Gabriel, with a flick of his fingers, cleansed all the mess away, resting his head on Lucifer's still heaving chest.

"I may have fucked countless creatures for a thrill, but no one or, to be honest, nothing has ever made me feel like that, Gabe. I am officially yours, heart and soul... Always."

"Well, I have been waiting a million lifetimes to show you exactly how much I have longed for you. I hope you felt it in every breath."

"We have always been connected by spirit," Lucifer agreed. "Now, we are connected by the body as well. I am yours, and you are mine."

"Always."

Gabriel watched Lucifer sleeping on his sofa. Pillows were scattered on the floor, and the silence was only slightly marred by the demon's peaceful breathing.

It was only the day before that such a sight would have been unheard of - a demon in the celestial office, and not just any demon, but *the* demon. The Lord of the Underworld was lying naked on the couch of the Lord of the… what… *Over*world??

Betrayals, mating's, transgressions, forgiveness. All acts of the past were now balanced out, ready for new victories and the inevitable fuck ups in the future.

Gabriel walked to his expansive window and looked out among the clouds. Funny how they looked the same. He was now mated, together with the one he had wanted and desired for so very long. His entire existence was defined by what he didn't have. Now that he had it, after long fucking last, he thought for sure everything would look different.

The clouds were the same. The sky too. He touched his arm and even gave it a pinch.

"Are you checking that this isn't a dream?" Lucifer asked as he wrapped his arms around Gabriel.

"It feels like it could be," Gabriel replied, "a dream come true, maybe."

"I envy you. That first-time-post-sex-glow. Sadly, no matter how fucking brilliant you were last night, I can't ever get that back."

"Apparently, it's not my first time. Not with you, not with anyone."

"So long to the 40-million-year-old virgin," Lucifer joked, "and hello to the best mate a fella could ask for."

They stood arm in arm, looking out onto the vast sky. Gabriel knew some things wouldn't be changing.

"We've got a lot to do," he said to Lucifer. "There are still so many angels and demons to be mated."

"We have five pairs on the list done," Lucifer nodded in agreement. "It will be a big fucking job."

"There's going to be dramas, resistance, complaining…"

"Betrayals, transgressions, forgiveness," the demon concurred. "Nothing new under the sun."

"Except us," Gabriel whispered as he nibbled on Lucifer's ear.

"And your angel spunk pulling the hairs on the inside of my thighs," the demon said. "Do you have showers up here, or is it all snapping fingers and waving wands?"

"Sorry, I thought I got all that when we'd finished."

Gabriel snapped his fingers, and the two were standing in a large, spacious shower stall. "Now show me where you feel sticky," he said as the water came down on the two of them, warm and soft, creating a cocoon neither one of them left for hours.

Chapter sixteen

The sign outside Club AZ read "Closed for Private Function."

It was a Monday night, so it wouldn't have been terribly busy anyway. Zagan and Anael were sure to staff the night with demons and angels only; no humans were to get within a hundred yards of the place. In addition, sentinels were set up on the perimeter to dissuade any curious onlookers and redirect them accordingly.

Inside, the music was pumping, and the dance floor was packed. Citizens of both the heavenly realm and the dark Underworld were mixing and mingling freely. Some a bit too freely, but why not? It was a party.

The gathering's purpose was to celebrate Lucifer and Gabriel's union, but since the archangel preferred to keep a very low profile, it was simply touted as a huge bash for angels and demons.

In addition to Zagan and Anael, all the original five mated pairs were on hand, dressed to the nines. They knew why they were there, and everyone paid their respects and passed on their congratulations to the newest - some would say the happiest - couple there.

"I knew the two of you would find each other eventually," Anael shouted above the din. "Once I saw the cord that bound you to one another, it was only a matter of time."

"Yes, well… Time is one thing we each have a shit ton of," Lucifer yelled as he downed another glass of champagne. He gave Gabriel's hand a squeeze as the archangel sipped his tea and kept a smile pasted on his face.

He was happy to be with Lucifer, and it was always a pleasure to see his angels flourishing with such joy, but he hated large parties with a passion. All Gabriel wanted to do was slip out the back door, Lucifer in tow, and head home, have sex, or maybe just watch a movie on Netflix, or both, and fall asleep in quiet bliss.

"You make a great pair," Michael shouted into Gabe's ear. "Honestly. Well done, my friend. I wish you all the happiness in the world."

"In the fucking universe," Orobas added. "The world's too small for the likes of these two."

Raziel and Botis were commandeering the dance floor, the angel's wings sprouting out and wrapping themselves around his demon whenever the dance tempo slowed down.

Uriel and Haures were huddled together at a table, laughing with Zagan, who had just arrived with another tray of drinks. Raphael was seated there as well, his eyes rolling around in their sockets as Seir administered what looked like the granddaddy of all back rubs.

Gabriel sat back and crossed his arms, enjoying the fruits of his labor. But he was tired and wanted to go.

"Just one night," Lucifer shouted in his ear, seemingly able to read Gabe's thoughts. "I promise not to make it a habit."

Gabriel nodded, putting down his tea cup and lifting his champagne flute up in an agreeable gesture of solidarity. It was still full, but Lucifer dumped the bottle over top of it anyway, causing the bubbly to spill down the sides.

Gabe waved his free hand to clean up the mess, and the entire bar froze instantly. The music, the lights, the demons, and the angels... all became a silent gallery of statues.

"Come on, Gabe," Lucifer moaned, clearly immune to the spell, "what the actual fuck? Can't we have just one night of fun?"

"It wasn't me," Gabriel protested, also plainly able to move and speak. "I was only trying to tidy up your spill so Zagan wouldn't-"

But his voice was silenced as the loud reverberation of a mighty bell sounded out, bouncing off the walls, ceiling, and floor. It was deafening.

"Oh fuck," Lucifer whispered.

"My lovely children," the familiar voice echoed and boomed, "how it warms me to see them all getting along so well. Angels and demons enjoying each other as equals. I couldn't ask for more."

"Good to know." Lucifer raised his glass ironically and winked at Gabriel. "Nice chatting with you. Come again soon."

Gabriel sent his mate a dirty look, trying to hush him, and Lucifer sucked his lips in over his teeth in deference.

"To what do we owe the pleasure of your visit, my Lord?" Gabriel loudly said.

"Such an ass-kisser," Lucifer whispered as he planted his hands on Gabriel's firm tush.

"Oh, nothing special," the Master replied, "just wondering when you two might be getting around to my directive."

Lucifer pulled his mouth away from Gabriel's ear and furrowed his brow in confusion.

"Your directive?" he called. "Maybe you haven't noticed, oh Absent-Minded-One, but we've been working our asses off fulfilling your fucking directive since we spoke with you in that little church. All six of the original mating's have now occurred, including the two of us, even though we didn't know we were on the list at the time."

"Are we missing something, my liege?" Gabriel added.

A loud 'tsk tsk tsk' thundered around the frozen bar.

"Nothing like getting scolded by the Master Micromanager," Lucifer said quietly to Gabe.

"The mating of the original six has been achieved, yes," said the voice, "but that was not my directive."

"I'm sorry, my liege…" Gabriel stuttered, flustered now. How he hated making mistakes at work. "Has balance not been restored as you desired?"

"Oh yes, there's that," the Voice conceded, "lots of balance now. Very good, very good. Balance for days. Heaps of balance. Well done." The voice took on a sharp, almost angry edge for the next bit: "But have you forgotten *why* I wanted some sense of balance restored in the first place?"

"Just skip to the chase, oh Great Tower of Babbling On," Lucifer snapped. "I'd like to finish my party and still have time to mount your man here before becoming a Demon of Dementia. So, what is it you want?"

"As I said before," the voice continued, "Humans have all but forgotten our existence and care only for how much they can cram into their brief lives. Both angels and demons are being ignored in their efforts to save or tempt, and I—

"Will. Not. Have. It." Lucifer cut him off. "Yeah, yeah, yeah. That rings a bell."

"So, what would you have us do?" Gabriel asked tentatively. He wanted to know the answer like he wanted a hot needle jabbed into his nuts.

"Whatever it takes," the Master thundered. "Now that you're all working together and have love as the wind beneath your wings, passion fueling your fires, I want my precious children to be reminded that you're *there*. That I'm *here*."

"Old school approach, or are you thinking something new?" Lucifer asked, drawn to the possibility of creating mischief in the world again.

"Surprise me. Miracles. Sightings. Plagues. Pandemics. Maybe a virgin birth or two? We haven't really done much in that way for a couple thousand years. I think it's time to shake things up a bit. Don't you?"

"Couldn't agree more," Lucifer cheered enthusiastically.

"Thy will be done," Gabriel said with a reluctant bow of his head.

The deafening clang of a bell sounded once more, signaling the end of the meeting, and in an instant, the bar came back to life.

Gabriel tossed his teacup to the floor and downed his glass of champagne instead.

"Look at you go," Lucifer smiled as he

refilled the flute. "An angel after my own heart."

"Not the organ I had in mind," Gabriel said, squeezing Lucifer's inner thigh, "but it's a good place to start."

"Tomorrow," Lucifer pleaded. "We'll start tomorrow. Tonight's for us."

"As you wish," the archangel murmured with a smile. "As you wish."

Epilogue

A scroll came in and landed with a thump on Gabriel's desk, pulling him away from Lucifer's intent gaze. It is hard to say how long they had been caught in each other, but time was a fickle beast, and it really didn't matter much to the pair of love birds most days.

"What on earth do Head Office want with us now? Time to bring down a plague of feral cats in Boston, is it?" Lucifer teased.

"Now, now, Luc, I'm sure it's nothing as vulgar as feral cats," Gabriel, tore his gaze away from Lucifer's face and twirled the scroll in his hands.

"We don't have to open it, you know; I would happily file it for you in the pits, we can pretend it never arrived."

Gabriel hoped his mate was joking, but a part of him knew there was a ring of truth to the words. Since the Master's voice had crashed their party, the two of them had been slightly on edge. Gabriel knew it was only a matter of time until a plan was sent to them for the commencement of phase two in the grand directive to have the humans reminded of the celestial world.

Plagues and earthquakes were not the solution, not in modern times as they were common already. But neither he nor Lucifer had been able to come up with a better plan. They also were at odds with how they felt the revival should look. Gabriel was, of course, a fan of miracles, healings, and feeding the poor. While Lucifer felt it would be more 'fun' to bring upon the humans a plague of leeches or zombies. Either way, having a scroll from Head Office didn't do anything for Gabriel's nerves.

"Let's just open it and see what they have to say, it might be enlightening," Gabriel managed the words with a small smile.

Official Head Office Report of Phase One of the Master's Grand Directive.

Approved by the Master before sending.

The Honorable Archangel Gabriel, Right Hand, and Voice of the Master and Lucifer, Exorbitant Ruler of the Underworld, were hereby given the task of successfully collaborating and bringing about the matings of six Angels and/or Archangels with High-Ranking Demons from the Underworld.

The sole purpose of this report is to critique their efforts and provide commentary if the aforementioned have been successful in reinstating balance in the universe.

Mating One

Raziel, Angel of Secrets with Demon Botis, Ruler of Sixty Legions.

It has been noted that despite some peculiar and unexpected mishaps occurring between fellow Angels, Raziel and Botis have been able to find a way to come together. Raziel is continuing to help the celestial world with finding old documents and precious artifacts and has conducted some exemplary work as Keeper of Secrets with Botis as his right-hand demon. Botis has maintained the command of his sixty legions, and it is said that all his troops have developed a respect, and some would say an adoration of Raziel due to his authority and grace in handling tough situations. Botis continues to grow and develop in his capacity to show care and attentiveness to his angel. They certainly seem to bring out the best in each other.

Status: Successfully mated with Head Office, and the Underworld mutually benefitted.

Mating Two

Anael Angel of Love, Passion, and Sexuality with King Zagan, Commander of the Legions of the Damned.

It has been noted by Head Office that after a short period of time in which the Angel Anael was not completing a satisfactory amount of connections, his quota has almost doubled since his mating to Zagan. The mere sight of the pair of them walking hand in hand is bringing joy, happiness, and connectivity to those that see them. It has been said that Anael's aura has increased in size, and his ability to see the threads that bind the humans to one another has increased by fifteen percent. King Zagan continues to run a tight ship in the Underworld, and there has been minimal incidence of inter legion fighting since the pair have been mated. It would appear that Zagan has added to Anael's ability to fulfill his mission on earth and that Anael has bought a calming and loving presence into the Underworld. They seem to be a wonderful fit.

Status: Successfully mated with Head Office, and the Underworld mutually benefitted.

Mating Three

The Angel Uriel, Muse to the World and Haures, Lord of the Souls of the Damned.

After a slow start and a somewhat tumultuous period of time concerning the soul known as Seth Turner, a satisfactory outcome was achieved for both parties. Head Office gained a magnificent and talented soul, and the Underworld offered refuge to a damned soul. Uriel continues to spread his love, kindness, and inspiration to those who find themselves in darkness, and Haures, the ever polite and remarkably honest Demon, continues with his remarkable and challenging work with the damned souls. He has developed some new routines which ensure timely rehabilitation opportunities for those who still hold the propensity for change and acceptable solutions for those souls who are unable to be rectified. The pairing seems to have resulted in both parties continuing with their roles in a heightened state of accomplishment.

Status: Successfully mated with Head Office, and the Underworld mutually benefitted.

Mating Four

Raphael, Archangel of Healing and Seir, the Finder of Lost Things and Demon of the Damned.

After their most advantageous and

successful first collaborative quest to retrieve the sacred trumpets associated with the end of times, Raphael and Seir have been traveling the globe simultaneously retrieving lost treasures, healing the hurt, and retrieving damned souls. They seamlessly intertwine their unique skillsets to ensure both the roles of both parties can continue to expand and bring forth impeccable results. The Archangel Raphael was able to continue with his role as the Angel of Travel in combination with his role as the Angel of Healing as he and the Demon Seir both enjoy traveling now they have companionship to share the journey with. Seir is able to collect souls from a much wider global net which is bringing about better efficiency with soul collection in the Underworld.

Status: Successfully mated with Head Office, and the Underworld mutually benefitted.

Mating Five

Michael the Archangel of Protection and Lord Orobas, Leader of Twenty Legions of the Underworld.

Both played vital roles in protecting the Lord of the Underworld when he was at his most vulnerable. The pair showed creativity, loyalty, and dedication to both celestial plains. This pairing illustrated the shared importance and how collaboration can truly bring about miraculous results. Carmine assisted Michael when he was in trouble in the Underworld, and Raphael and Gabriel helped Orobas when he was in trouble on earth. True teamwork. As a pairing, Michael has been able to learn some valuable skills from Orobas and instigate some impeccable new protection measures in order to protect those who require it. Orobas is reveling in his creative pursuits and bringing joy to the people of earth with his works. Whilst managing to continue to manage his twenty legions of souls in the Underworld, his reports indicate the lowest levels of internal violence in history.

Status: Successfully mated with Head Office, and the Underworld mutually benefitted.

Mating Six

Archangel Gabriel, Right Hand and Voice for the Master and The Lord of the Underworld, Lucifer.

While many of the events leading up to the pairing have been challenging to locate, the Master asserts the how was not relevant to the writing of this report. The report will, however, note a huge increase in productivity in both offices held by the two aforementioned parties. Gabriel is maintaining order and vigilance within his office, and Lucifer continues to maintain the Underworld within acceptable standards. A recent influx in souls needing allocation has meant that the pair have been working closely together to ensure adequate staffing and provisions for each soul has been made regardless of their destination. The long-awaited joining of these two celestial beings has been celebrated in all camps, and Head Office has no doubt they will do great things together.

Status: Successfully mated with Head Office, and the Underworld mutually benefitted.

In conclusion, the Master speaks of how happy it makes him to see everyone getting along, angels and demons enjoying each other as equals. He couldn't ask for more from the first stage in his directive, and he looks forward to what can be achieved next.

Lucifer and Gabriel have been successful in ensuring all five previous pairings were conducted with dignity and care. Each pairing was given adequate time post-mating to consolidate their relationship and get to know one another, which ensures higher success and fulfillment of destinies.

Lucifer and Gabriel would do well to remember that despite the magnitude of their roles, they, too, will be afforded the opportunity to have a break and consolidate their pairing.

The Master will reach out to you both upon your return from your leave to discuss phase two of his directive. But in the meantime, enjoy your break, and thank you for doing your valuable part in ensuring the increase of balance in the delicate world we serve.

Kind Regards and Ample Blessings

Head Office

"Well, I could certainly call that enlightening Gabe darling," Lucifer chuckled after Gabriel had finished reading the report.

"It sounds to me like Head Office, in some strange way giving us some acknowledgment of a job well done," Gabriel said finding it easier to smile now he knew the contents of the scroll.

"It sounds to me like Head Office is also telling us we can take a holiday, and I, for one, would not want to be a disappointment to our intrepid leaders." Lucifer had mischief written all over his gorgeous face.

"What on earth would we do on a

holiday?" Gabriel knew that was something he'd never done before.

"Oh, I am sure we can find plenty of things to keep us occupied, my angelic lover." Lucifer wrapped Gabriel in his arms as he spoke and started planting several kisses along his neck and jawline.

"You know what, I think you are absolutely right, a holiday is exactly what we need. I'll get some things organized on my end, and we can take leave from tomorrow." Gabriel squirmed halfheartedly but didn't pull away from Lucifer's embrace.

"You know what, babe, screw being organized and making a plan. Send a message out to the masses that we are away, and we will be back… when we get back."

Gabriel looked into Lucifer's eyes for a full minute, not saying a word, until, at last, a smile broke out on his face.

"As. You. Wish."

The End.

I didn't leave much of a note in book five as this one was already written, and I knew I would be putting it out as soon as I could. Those of you who have been following this series have been very patient as there was quite a gap there for a while between books two and three, so I thank you for sticking with me, even when I took a while getting these last ones out.

I will not be writing anymore Balance books. They were a series I wanted to write for myself, but they were a departure from what I normally write, and many readers have noticed that difference in style and content and aren't keen. Which is fair enough, but if you're reading this, thank you so much for coming along for the ride with my angels and demons. I hope you enjoyed Lucifer and Gabriel's story and how things were left. I can assure they have a very, very long happy ever after to enjoy.

Books that are coming up – most notably Loki's story from the Gods series. I started that book three times before I got to a story line that I think suits one of my favorite gods, so that will hopefully be out in May (2022). I am also writing the Tangled Tentacles Series with JP Sayle, and the sequel to Illuminate is also next on my list. I have written a couple of other projects that I am looking forward to putting out (once they are finished) but I will tell you more about them as they get closer to being released.

As we all settle into our new normal, I am giving my muse a bit more free rein to see what comes from doing that and I'm excited to see what comes from that. In the meantime, as sales are being decimated by changes to the Amazon policies and the way readers can buy their books, I would truly appreciate it if you can leave me a review at your place of purchase. Believe me when I tell you it truly does help.

I do believe the pandemic has made many of us rethink the ways we live our lives, and perhaps helped us focus on those things that are truly important. My love of writing has never stopped, and won't, but I am looking forward to moving closer to my children real soon and learning to downsize and not worry so much about 'stuff'. One of the things I do hang onto is my love and appreciation for all of you – my readers who are also my friends and family. Thank you so much for simply being there – it means the world to me.

Stay safe, stay well, and hug the ones you love.

Huge hugs,

Lisa xxx

About the Author

Lisa Oliver lives in the wilds of New Zealand, sharing her home with her two Rotty dogs, Zeus and Hades. They can often be found, sleeping around her office chair as she taps out the stories she loves. With over seventy paranormal MM (and MMM) titles to her name so far, she shows no signs of slowing down.

When Lisa is not writing, she is usually reading with a cup of tea always at hand. Her grown children and grandchildren sometimes try and pry her away from the computer and have found that the best way to do it is to promise her chocolate. Lisa will do anything for chocolate.

Lisa loves to hear from her readers and other writers (I really do, lol). You can catch up with her on any of the social media links below.

Facebook –
http://www.facebook.com/lisaoliverauthor

Official Author page –
https://www.facebook.com/LisaOliverManloveAuthor/

My new private teaser group -
https://www.facebook.com/groups/540361549650663/

My MeWe Group - http://mewe.com/join/lisa_olivers_paranormal_pack

And Instagram - https://www.instagram.com/lisa_oliver_author/

My blog - http://www.paranormalgayromance.com

Twitter – http://www.twitter.com/wisecrone333

Youtube (I am so awful at this lol, but it makes me laugh) - https://www.youtube.com/channel/UCuPx1orrUiUHt_ECNaX8SWw and

TikTok - https://www.tiktok.com/@lisaoliver135 (These could be easier to watch because the videos are shorter lol)

And now I have a new store where you can buy my art, t-shirt designs and custom swag items - https://www.etsy.com/nz/shop/LisasCreationsNZ

Email me directly at yoursintuitively@gmail.com.

Other Books By Lisa/Lee Oliver

Please note, I have now marked the books that contain mpreg and MMM for those of you who don't like to read those type of stories. Hope that helps ☺

Cloverleah Pack

Book 1 – The Reluctant Wolf – Kane and Shawn

Book 2 – The Runaway Cat – Griff and Diablo

Book 3 – When No Doesn't Cut It – Damien and Scott

Book 3.5 – Never Go Back – Scott and Damien's Trip and a free story about Malacai and Elijah

Book 4 – Calming the Enforcer – Troy and Anton

Book 5 – Getting Close to the Omega – Dean and Matthew

Book 6 – Fae for All – Jax, Aelfric and Fafnir (M/M/M)

Book 7 – Watching Out for Fangs –Josh and Vadim

Book 8 – Tangling with Bears – Tobias, Luke and Kurt (M/M/M)

Book 9 – Angel in Black Leather – Adair and Vassago

Book 9.5 – Scenes from Cloverleah – four short stories featuring the men we've come to love

Book 10 – On the Brink – Teilo, Raff and Nereus (M/M/M)

Book 11 – Don't Tempt Fate – Marius and Cathair

Book 12 – My Treasure to Keep – Thomas and Ivan

Book 13 – Home is Where the Heart is – Wesley and Castor

The Gods Made Me Do It (Cloverleah spin off series)

Book One - Get Over It – Madison and Sebastian's story

Book Two - You've Got to be Kidding – Poseidon and Claude (mpreg)

Book Three – Don't Fight It – Lasse and Jason

Book Four – Riding the Storm – Thor and Orin (mpreg elements [Jason from previous book gives birth in this one])

Book Five – I Can See You – Artemas and Silvanus (mpreg elements – Thor gives birth in this one)

Book Six – Someone to Hold Me – Hades and Ali (mpreg elements but no birth)

Book Seven – You'll Know in Your Heart – Baby and Owen (mpreg)

Book Eight – Worth It – Zeus and Paulie (mpreg)

Book Nine – When Three Points Collide – Ra, Kirill and Arvyn (M/M/M) (mpreg elements, no birth)

Book Ten – Special Enough – Odin and Evan

Book Eleven – Reconciliation: Seth's Story – (Seth and Luka) (mpreg is a small part of this story)

Book Twelve – Being Loki - coming May/June 2022 – I'm writing this one now.

The Necromancer's Smile (This is a trilogy series under the name The Necromancer's Smile where the main couple, Dakar and Sy are the focus of all three books – these cannot be read as standalone).

Book One – Dakar and Sy – The Meeting

Book Two – Dakar and Sy – Family affairs

Book Three – Dakar and Sy – Taking Care of Business

Bound and Bonded Series

Book One – Don't Touch – Levi and Steel

Book Two – Topping the Dom – Pearson and Dante

Book Three – Total Submission – Kyle and Teric

Book Four – Fighting Fangs – Ace and Devin

Book Five – No Mate of Mine – Roger and Cam

Book Six – Undesirable Mate – Phillip and Kellen

Stockton Wolves Series

Book One – Get off My Case – Shane and Dimitri

Book Two – Copping a Lot of Sin – Ben, Sin and Gabriel (M/M/M)

Book Three – Mace's Awakening – Mace and Roan

Book Four – Don't Bite – Trent and Alexi

Book Five – Tell Me the Truth – Captain Reynolds and Nico (mpreg)

Alpha and Omega Series

Book One – The Biker's Omega – Marly and Trent

Book Two – Dance Around the Cop – Zander and Terry

Book Three – Change of Plans - Q and Sully

Book Four – The Artist and His Alpha – Caden and Sean

Book Five – Harder in Heels – Ronan and Asaph

Book Six – A Touch of Spring – Bronson and Harley

Book Seven – If You Can't Stand the Heat – Wyatt and Stone (Previously published in an anthology)

Book Eight – Fagin's Folly – Fagin and Cooper

Book Nine – The Cub and His Alphas – Daniel, Zeke and Ty (MMM)

Book Ten – The One Thing Money Can't Buy – Cari and Quaid

Book Eleven – Precious Perfection – Devyn and Rex

Book Twelve – More Than a Handful - Karl and Tanner

Spin off from The Biker's Omega – BBQ, Bikes, and Bears – Clive and Roy

Balance – Angels and Demons

The Viper's Heart – Raziel and Botis

Passion Punched King – Anael and Zagan

Soul Deep – Uriel and Haures

Found – Raphael and Seir

Demon Masks and Angel Wings – Michael and Orobas

Love Before Time – Lucifer and Gabriel

Arrowtown

A Tiger's Tale – Ra and Seth (mpreg)

Snake Snack – Simon and Darwin (mpreg)

Liam's Lament – Liam Beau and Trent (MMM) (Mpreg)

Doc's Deputy – Deputy Joe and Doc (Mpreg)

Cam's Chance – Cam and Fergus (Mpreg)

Stone Cold Obsidian – Dian and Kee (Mpreg)

Brutus's Surprise – Brutus and Heath

City Dragons

Dragon's Heat – Dirk and Jon

Dragon's Fire – Samuel and Raoul

Dragon's Tears – Byron and Ivak

The Magic Users of Greenford – a new trilogy.

Book One - Illuminate

Quirk of Fate

Summons – Edward and Mammon

Reggie's Reasons – Reggie and Dirkin

Hellhound Collar Series

Collar and Scruff (Prequel) – Raoul and Jason (Freebie giveaway YBBB)

Better Than Sweets (Book 1) – Java and Cyril

Tangled Tentacles – in Collaboration with JP Sayle

Book one – Alexi – Alexi and Danik

Book 2 – Victor – Azim and Victor (mpreg)

Book 3 – Todd – (MMM mpreg) Todd, Lucas and Ki

Standalone:

I Should've Stayed Home: Irwin's Story – Part of the Nocturne Bay collab series – Irwin and Kolton

The Fall of the Fairy Tale Prince – Charlie and Lex (A spin off from Dancing Around the Cop and Change of Plans in the A&O series)

Stay True to Me – Con and Ven

Rowan and the Wolf – Rowan and Shadow

Bound by Blood – Max and Lyle – (a spin off from Cloverleah Pack #7)

The Power of the Bite – Dax and Zane

One Wrong Step – Robert and Syron

Uncaged – Carlin and Lucas (Shifter's Uprising in conjunction with Thomas Oliver)

Also under the penname Lee Oliver/Lisa Oliver

Northern States Pack Series

Book One – Ranger's End Game – Ranger and Aiden

Book Two – Cam's Promise – Cam and Levi

Book Three – Under Sean's Protection – Sean and Kyle

Book Four – Newton's Law – Newton and Tron